Enid Blyton

THE FLYAWAY BROOMSTICK

and other tales of magic

Illustrated by
Paul Crompton
and Joyce Johnson

World International Publishing Limited
Manchester

Published in Great Britain by World International
Publishing Limited,
An Egmont Company, Egmont House, PO Box 111,
Great Ducie Street,
Manchester M60 3BL.
Printed in Italy.

British Library Cataloguing in Publication Data
Blyton, Enid 1897–1968
The flyaway broomstick and other tales of magic.
I. Title
823.912 [J]

ISBN 0–7498–0296–0

Cover illustration by Robin Lawrie

Contents

Enid Blyton

Enid Blyton was born in London in 1897. Her childhood was spent in Beckenham, Kent, and as a child she began to write poems, stories and plays. She trained to be a teacher but she devoted her whole life to being a children's author. Her first book was a collection of poems for children, published in 1922. In 1926 she began to write a weekly magazine for children called *Sunny Stories*, and it was here that many of her most popular stories and characters first appeared. The magazine was immensely popular and in 1953 it became *The Enid Blyton Magazine*.

She wrote more than 600 books for children and many of her most popular series are still published all over the world. Her books have been translated into over 30 languages. Enid Blyton died in 1968.

The flyaway broomstick

There was once a most annoying pixie called Poppo, who lived in Wobble Village on the borders of Fairyland. He was annoying because he was always borrowing things and never returning them.

"It is such a nuisance," said one small pixie to another. "That naughty Poppo borrowed my kettle yesterday, and now he says he didn't. So I have had to buy a new kettle!"

"And I had to buy a new set of dusters," complained another. "I hung mine out on the line, and Poppo came and borrowed them all without asking me. Then he said he hadn't, so I had to go out and spend all my money on some new ones."

"If only he wasn't so powerful," sighed a third. "But we daren't refuse him, or scold him, because he knows more magic than any of us."

"Yes, and do you remember how he turned little Sylfay into a worm because she told him he wasn't a borrower, he was a robber?" said the first one. "We can't do anything, you know."

But matters got so bad that the village knew they would have to do *something*. Poppo borrowed, or took without asking, all their nicest things. He would never give them back, and often said he had never had them at all. The little folk were in despair.

"I will go to the wise woman on top of Breezy Hill," said Chippy, the leader. "Perhaps she will be able to help us."

So he went off the next morning and told his tale to the old wise woman. She listened, and for a time

8

said nothing.

"You must be careful," she said. "This Poppo is quite a powerful pixie."

"I know," sighed Chippy. "But surely, oh wise woman, you can think of some way to stop him?"

The wise woman thought again. Then she smiled. She went to a cupboard, and took out a long broom.

"I have an idea," she said. "Take this broomstick home with you, Chippy. It once belonged to a witch, and it flies in the air. There is a flyaway spell hidden in it that will take twelve people for a flight and bring them back safely. But the thirteenth flight takes it to the witch it once belonged to, and she will keep for a servant the thirteenth rider."

"Ooh!" said Chippy, frightened. "Well, what are we to do?"

"Fly it in front of Poppo's house," said the wise woman. "Let twelve pixies, one after another, have a ride, and then stop. Put it somewhere so that Poppo can borrow it – and if he doesn't fly off to the witch, then I am no wise woman!"

Chippy grinned in delight, and hurried off to Wobble Village with the fine broomstick. He whispered all about it to the others, and in great glee they went to Poppo's cottage.

"I'll have first ride," said Chippy. He sat astride the broomstick and waited. Suddenly it rose into the air, circled round the tree-tops, shot up high, and then glided gently down to the ground again.

"Fine! Fine!" cried all the watching pixies.

"Someone else can have a turn now," said Chippy. He slid off, and another pixie leapt on. Up rose the broomstick again, and away it went over the tree-tops.

When the fifth ride was being taken, Chippy saw Poppo looking out of his window. Chippy grinned. Each of the pixies had a turn, but after the twelfth ride, Chippy stopped them.

"No more," he said. "It's tea-time. We must all go home. I must take my broom into my backyard now, and use it for its proper purpose – sweeping!"

Off they all went. Poppo watched them go. He badly wanted a ride, but he wasn't going to say so. No, he would go to Chippy to ask him for the loan of his broom, saying that he wanted to sweep out his backyard.

So after tea he put on his hat and went round to Chippy's cottage. Chippy was watching for him, for he felt sure he was coming.

"Good evening, Chippy," said Poppo. "Would you be so good as to lend me a broom?"

"Ha ha! You want to ride on it!" said Chippy, pointing his finger at him.

"Indeed I don't," said Poppo, looking offended. "I want to sweep my backyard."

"Well I warn you – if you ride on it you'll be taken off to the witch who owns it!" said Chippy, who felt it would not be fair to let Poppo have the broom without a warning. "No, Poppo – I think I won't lend it to you, after all."

Poppo scowled as he went off. Chippy watched him. Soon the mean little pixie returned by the back way, creeping quietly into the backyard, where he had spied the broom. He meant to take it without permission.

He ran off with it. Chippy whistled to his friends, and they all went softly after Poppo to watch what would happen.

"I said he wasn't to borrow it, and I warned him what would happen if he rode on it," said Chippy. "It will be his own fault if he is spirited away. He said he just wanted to sweep out his backyard."

The pixies peeped over the wall. Poppo had the broom by the kitchen door. He was looking at it carefully.

"All the other pixies had a ride, so I don't see why I shouldn't, too," said

Poppo. "That warning of Chippy's was all made up – he just said it so that I shouldn't have a nice ride like the others!"

He jumped on the broomstick. At once it rose into the air. It circled three times round the tree-tops, rose very high – and then went off like a streak of lightning to the west, where the old witch lived!

"Ooh! He's gone!" cried the pixies.

So he had; and as he never came back I suppose the witch took him for her servant. He is probably there still. The pixies were delighted to be rid of him. They went to his cottage and took away all the things that Poppo had borrowed and forgotten to return.

"Good old wise woman!" said Chippy. "I'll bake her a cake this Saturday!"

He did – and she was simply delighted.

The magic duster

Heyho the goblin had made a magic duster. My word, he was proud of it too! Just a flick with that duster would make anything shine and glitter as brightly as the sun!

"I shall make some money out of this!" said Heyho to himself. "I'll go round and offer to polish when people are doing their spring-cleaning. They will find my magic duster very useful!"

So in the spring he went around to the pixies, elves, brownies and gnomes, and offered the use of his wonderful duster.

"Just a flick and all your silver will sparkle!" he said. "Just a rub and your old paint will shine like new! Just a touch and your floors will be polished enough to dance on all night long!"

Well, everyone borrowed that duster, you may be sure! Gobo the gnome borrowed it for his silver bowls and cups, the ones he had won for being the fastest runner in the village. Twinkle the elf borrowed it for her beautiful old furniture, and after a flick and a rub all her dark brown chairs and tables and stools glowed and shone in a marvellous manner.

"It certainly saves a lot of work," said Twinkle. "It would have taken me weeks to polish all my furniture properly."

Henny-Penny borrowed it to polish her chicks' beaks, and all the blackbirds did the same. Everybody had to pay Heyho a ten pence piece, so he soon became very rich.

And then the Queen heard of the magic duster, and she sent for Heyho. He was so proud when he got the message, and off he went to the palace.

Well, the Queen wanted a good deal done, and she hoped that the magic duster could do it.

"I want my beautiful old glasses and jugs polished," she said. "And I want all the windows done. And you might do the paint whilst you are here, and all the silver and gold plate, too."

So Heyho was quite busy for a day, for although he just had to flick here and there, there were a good many flicks to get through! Soon all the windows, the glasses, the silver and the gold, and the paint gleamed and shone and glowed. Everybody admired Heyho's work, and he began to get very vain and conceited.

"This is nothing to what I *can* do!" he said. "I'll do a few things that the Queen hasn't asked for, and you'll see how marvellous my duster is!"

"No, you mustn't do anything you have not been told to do," said the butler. Heyho grinned cheekily. He meant to do just exactly what he pleased!

Well, that night, when everyone was

in bed, he went to the golden thrones of the King and Queen and rubbed them lightly with his magic duster. How they shone! How they glittered! But, dear me, how slippery they were!

He flicked his duster over the beautiful wooden floors, and they too glowed. They were very slippery with the magic, and Heyho at once fell down three times before he managed to get into the hall.

And then, just for fun, he did a very naughty thing. He flicked his duster over all the boots and shoes lying in the kitchen for the kitchen-maid to clean the next morning! He meant to shine up the tops of the boots and shoes, but he knew quite well that his duster would send its magic shine on to the bottoms of the shoes as well; and, dear me, nobody likes slippery shoes to walk on!

Then he went to bed, wondering what everyone would say the next day.

Things happened quickly the next

morning. The two footmen who carried coal to make the fires in the Queen's breakfast-room had to walk along the slippery floor. Down they went, and all the coal flew into every corner. The King and Queen woke up in a fright, and the King put on his dressing-gown and went to see what was the matter.

Of course, as soon as he stepped on the slippery stairs his feet flew from

under him, and he went down with a dreadful bump!

How he roared! And plenty of other people roared too, when they found that they couldn't walk on the gleaming, slippery floors! Down went breakfast-trays, down went brushes and brooms and pans, crash – thud – bang!

The butler ordered carpets to be nailed on to the floors, but, good gracious me, things didn't seem very much better, for as soon as anyone wore the boots or shoes that Heyho had rubbed with his magic duster, down they went, whether they walked on carpet or wooden floor! They simply could not stand on their slippery soles.

The butler complained to the King and Queen. "Someone's been playing a bad joke," he said. "And I think I know who it is!"

"I think I do too," said the King grimly. "Call everyone, and the Queen and I will find the joker and punish him."

So in a little while all the servants stood in the great hall, and the King and Queen walked to their golden thrones.

But they couldn't sit on them! Heyho had made them so slippery with his magic duster that as soon as the King and the Queen sat on the polished seats they slid off them, and sat on the ground!

So they had to stand, and the King's frown was like a black thunder-cloud. It made Heyho tremble when he was brought before all the servants and before Their Majesties too!

"Take hold of this silly goblin and throw him up into the moon," commanded the King. "I'm tired of him!"

Heyho hadn't time to squeal or to beg for mercy. Two strong footmen took hold of him, swung him in front of the open window two or three times, and then let go! Up he went in the air, up and up and up! But he didn't quite reach the moon, for it happened to be rather far away that day. So he fell back to earth again, and dropped into a hawthorn hedge which pricked him hard, but held him fast so that he wasn't hurt much.

All round him was a golden buttercup-field and a little elf was patiently polishing the cups as they opened. It was a long, long job. Heyho watched for a moment. Then he took out his magic duster and flung it to the elf.

"Take it!" he said. "It's got me into dreadful trouble, and I'd better not use it any more. But you're welcome to it. Goodbye, I'm off to the land of Never-Never, where I hope I'll never-never get into trouble again!"

So off he went – and he's never-never been heard of since. But the elf uses that duster every summer. She just flicks it round a buttercup-field, and her work is done! Every buttercup shines as if it had been well polished and gleams like gold. Pick one and look into it. Isn't it beautifully polished?

The six red wizards

Once upon a time there were six red wizards. They lived in a castle together, and dressed in red cloaks and red pointed hats. Their eyes, however, were as green as the eyes of cats, and it was said that all six wizards could see in the dark.

Their castle stood right in the middle of the town of Mumble, where lived many merry little folk – but since the coming of the wizards, the people of Mumble had not been quite so merry as before.

They were afraid of the red wizards. They didn't like their children to play near the castle in case their shouts annoyed the wizards. They didn't like to hold dances on the village green in case the wizards came and stopped them. They wished the wizards would go away.

But this was just what the six red wizards wouldn't do! They were very comfortable where they were, and, as they were planning a great deal of magic in their castle, they were not going to disturb themselves for anyone.

Now they had a servant called Fum, an ugly, bad-tempered little creature. He had served them for many years, and then, one day, when he had made them an apple pie in which he had put salt in mistake for sugar, the six wizards flew into a temper with him.

"Box his ears!" said one, and his ears were boxed.

"Spank him hard!" said another, and he was spanked.

Fum let out a howl of rage, picked up the apple pie, and threw it at the wizards. It spilt all over them. Whilst they were wiping their eyes, Fum ran

from the room and disappeared.

They hunted all over the castle for him, but he was gone. He knew quite well that he would be turned into a blade of grass or a dead leaf if they found him – so he had quickly picked up his little bag and off he had run.

He was full of hate for his six unkind masters. He went into the town of Mumble and made his way to the big house where the mayor of the town lived. He knocked at the door and asked to see him.

"His Highness will see you in ten minutes," said the butler. Fum was taken into a little room, and there he waited for ten minutes. Then His Highness the mayor of Mumble came in, looking very grand and important.

But he didn't look so grand and important after he had heard what Fum had to say – for Fum gave away all the wizards' secrets, and frightened the mayor very much.

"The wizards are making a marvellous spell," said Fum. "It is nearly finished. When this spell is used, a million soldiers will spring from nothing, and at the wizards' command will march all through Fairyland, destroying every town. They cannot be stopped, for no one can kill them. They will banish the King and Queen, and make everyone their slaves. The wizards themselves will sit on six red thrones and rule the whole of Fairyland."

"Now this is dreadful!" cried the mayor, his cheeks turning pale. "Are you sure of this, Fum?"

THE SIX RED WIZARDS

"Quite," said Fum. "Listen, Your Highness. I will take you and three others by a secret way into the castle, and you shall peep through a hole and see the wizards at work, making soldiers out of nothing."

So that night the mayor and three others were taken by Fum through a secret passage into the castle, and peeped through a hole in the wall. And there, sure enough, they saw one of the wizards standing in a chalk circle, chanting magic words and making soldiers appear out of nothing.

The next day the mayor called a meeting and told the townspeople all he had seen. He sent a message to the King and Queen themselves, and soon all Fairyland was full of fear.

Then a messenger was sent all through the land proclaiming that if anyone could force the wizards to leave the country, he would be made a Prince and should marry the Princess.

Now it so happened that a wandering

seller of lamps and candles heard the messenger proclaiming his news, and he marvelled to think that almost in a night a man such as he might become a Prince and marry a Princess.

The candle-seller went to a pond and looked at himself in the water. He saw looking back at him a young and merry face, with twinkling eyes, and black curly hair.

"Now," he said, "why should not I be the man who shall become Prince and win the lovely Princess for his wife?"

With that he made up his mind to try. He journeyed to Mumble and soon came to the castle of the six red wizards. He stood looking over the wall, wondering what to do.

"Beware!" said an old woman, coming by. "Over a hundred young men have tried to defeat the wizards this week — and not one of them has succeeded. Do you see that big cage in that window over there, full of birds? Well, the wizards turned each young man into a bird, and there they will be for the rest of their lives."

"Well, I am going to try my luck," said the candle-seller, and he knocked boldly at the castle gate. It swung open, and he went in, carrying his candles and his lamps with him.

He climbed a long flight of steps up to the castle door, which slowly opened as he approached it. He stepped through and found himself in a great hall. The six red wizards sat in a row at one end. The young man went up to them and bowed.

"Would you buy new lamps or candles?" he asked. "I have come from afar to sell my wares."

"We want no lamps or candles," said one wizard. "But we need a servant. Do you know anything of magic?"

"I have learnt a little," said the candle-seller.

"Do you work hard?" asked the second wizard.

"Yes, for I have done nothing else all

the days of my life," answered the young man.

"Then you shall be our servant," said the third wizard.

"Wait," said the young man. "I am only used to serving wise and powerful masters. I do not work for weaklings. Prove to me that you are learned in magic, and I will be your servant."

"Now this is a bold young man to talk so," said the fifth wizard, angrily.

"Not so," said the sixth. "It is all the better for us if he has been used to powerful masters. He will do our bidding well."

"Prove your power to me," said the candle-seller.

The wizards began to laugh among themselves, for never before had they met such a bold young man.

"Very well," said the first one. "We will show you what we can do."

They meant to frighten him and make him sorry for his bold words, but it was difficult to make him afraid, for he had one of the bravest hearts in the world. He did not tremble when with one accord the wizards turned into roaring lions, nor did he spring back when they changed into a torrent that rushed around his feet.

Then they changed into spiders and began to weave a web round him – but the young man laughed in scorn. They turned into eagles and flapped their wings about his head, but he only smiled. Last of all they made themselves very small and then suddenly very big – but not a shiver or a tremble could they get from the brave candle-seller.

"Ho!" he said, when the six wizards stood once more in front of him. "That is quite good magic you did – but it is easy to work the magic that you know. Do three things that I command you, and I will be your servant."

The six wizards frowned.

"What are your three things?" they demanded. "Have a care not to try us too far, bold candle-seller. You will

perhaps find yourself in the cage with those birds over there before very long."

"Then you will lose a good servant," said the young man. "Now these are my three tests. First, can you make yourselves invisible?"

The wizards laughed scornfully. They spread out their hands, said a curious magic word, and lo and behold! They had disappeared! Their chairs were empty!

"Very clever!" said the youth. The wizards suddenly appeared again, and sat down in their chairs.

"What is your second test?" they asked.

"The second test is – multiply yourselves by three!" said the youth. In a trice the wizards had turned into eighteen, and surrounded the youth in a ring. He didn't turn a hair, but waved his hand to tell them to become six again.

"Now your last test," said the wizards.

"Ah!" said the young man. "This is a

test that few wizards can do."

He set out six candles in candlesticks on a table. "Now," he said, "turn yourselves into the six flames of my candles!"

With a scornful laugh the wizards disappeared, and in a trice six red flames appeared at the top of the six candles, burning steadily.

"Ha!" said the young man mockingly. "Very clever!" Then, lightly and easily, he blew at each candle in turn. Puff! Out went one flame. Puff! Out went another. Puff! Out went a third. Puff! Puff! Puff! Out went the fourth, fifth and sixth – and where were the six wizards? Gone out with the candle-flames! They had had no time to take their own shapes again, and they were blown out for good. To this day no one has ever heard of them again.

"Ho ho!" laughed the young man. "That's the end of the red wizards! Now this castle is mine and all the treasure in it! Tomorrow I shall be made a Prince, and the lovely Princess will be mine!"

Then he noticed that the birds in the cage were all clamouring to be set free. He opened the cage door and they flew out. No sooner were they free than each bird disappeared and became the young man he had been before. Then one and all crowded round the candle-seller and swore to be his faithful servants.

What merry-making there was in the town of Mumble and in the whole of Fairyland that night! The news flew from place to place, and the King and Queen came themselves in great state to see the wonderful young man who had defeated the six powerful wizards.

And next day the wedding bells rang out merrily, for the Princess herself came to marry him. When she saw his twinkling eyes and black curly hair she was glad, and smiled at him. He smiled gaily at his lovely bride, and so with glad hearts they were married, and lived happily ever after.

A pins and needles spell

"We're going to have a meeting this afternoon to decide what to give Princess Peronel for a birthday present," said Whiskers, the brownie, to Jinks and Cheery.

"Well, don't ask old Meanie then," said Jinks. "He made an awful fuss last year, and wouldn't vote even a penny towards a present."

"And the little Princess is *such* a dear," said Cheery. "Always a smile and a wave for everyone. I vote we buy her a pair of dancing shoes for her nimble little feet, and get the Pixie Fly-High to fetch a couple of tiny stars from the sky, to put on the slippers' toes. Think how her feet would twinkle when she dances!"

"Now that's a really bright idea!" said Whiskers, pleased. "Bring it up at the meeting, Cheery. It's to be held in the Toadstool Wood, and Gobo is growing a few toadstools for us to sit on."

"Right. I'll tell the others," said Jinks. "But we *won't* ask old Meanie!"

They didn't ask Meanie – but he heard of the meeting, of course, and was very angry because he hadn't been invited. He went straight to Gobo, Jinks and Cheery.

"I shall come!" he said, "and what's more I shall talk the whole time, and tell you what nonsense it is to give presents to a rich Princess, and nobody else will get a word in!"

"You did that last time," said Gobo. "That's why we're not asking you to the meeting. You can't come if you're not asked."

"That's just where you're wrong!" said Meanie, fiercely. "I *shall* come.

I know where you're all meeting – in the Toadstool Wood!"

"I forbid you to come!" said Gobo, sternly. "And don't you dare to disobey – or I'll put a dreadful spell on you!"

"Don't be so silly," said Meanie. "*You* put a spell on *me*? Why, you couldn't put a spell on a beetle! What *sort* of spell, I'd like to know?"

"I might put a tick-tock spell on you," said Gobo. "So that you could only tick-tock like a clock, instead of speaking. Or a sleepy spell, so that you fell asleep. Or a pins and needles spell . . ."

"And what exactly is *that*?" said Meanie, mockingly. "I've never heard of it in my life – and neither have you, Gobo. This is all a bit of make-believe! Pins and needles spell, indeed!"

"A pins and needles spell is a spell that, quite suddenly, makes you feel as if there are pins and needles sticking into you!" said Gobo, solemnly. "It's very, very uncomfortable. I think I

will put that spell on you, Meanie –
and when *that* works, I'll put *another*
one on you – the tick-tock one, that
will make everyone laugh at you!"

And, to the surprise of Jinks and
Cheery, Gobo suddenly clapped his
hands and danced all round the
surprised Meanie, singing loudly.

"Here's a pins and needles spell,
Prick him, *jab him*,
Make him yell,
Here's a pins and needles SPELL!"

Meanie laughed. "Well? Where are
your pins and needles? *I* haven't felt
any! Don't try and make spells, Gobo
– you don't know anything about
them."

"Oh, the spell will only work if you
come and spoil our meeting," said Gobo,
solemnly. "Not unless. So keep away,
Meanie, unless you want suddenly to
feel jabbed and pricked all over!"

Meanie went off, still laughing. "I'll
come to the meeting all right," he

shouted back. "And I'll certainly tell you what I think about spending our money on Princesses!"

"Horrid fellow!" said Cheery. "Why, our little Princess Peronel is our great friend – we've watched her grow up from a tiny baby into the merriest child in the kingdom. Gobo, you shouldn't have said that spell – you *know* it won't work! You don't know any magic, and never have. You'll only make us look foolish this afternoon, when Meanie comes to the meeting, and no spell happens!"

"You wait and see," said Gobo. "There are more ways than one of making a spell happen. I can do spells without magic!"

"Rubbish!" said Jinks. "Well – we'll see you at the meeting. You've got to grow fifteen toadstools – sixteen, if Meanie comes, and I'm pretty certain he will."

That afternoon Gobo was very busy. He grew toadstool after toadstool for seats. He draped each one with little cloths that hung to the ground, for Gobo liked to do things well.

Then he disappeared into the ditch, and talked to someone there for a long time. Who was it? Ah, you wait and see! Anyway, the someone came to the ring of toadstools with him, and stood there patiently while Gobo draped *him* with a little cloth, too! He looked exactly like another seat.

The brownies began to come to the meeting in twos and threes. Gobo showed them to their seats. "No – don't sit *there*," he kept saying, pointing to one draped seat. "That's for Meanie, if he comes. It's a seat with a *pins and needles spell!*"

"Dear old Gobo – *you* can't make spells – you know you can't!" said Cheery. "Now, just don't say any more about pins and needles, for goodness sake."

Soon they were all sitting down, and the draped toadstool seats each held a brownie. Only one seat had no one on it – and that was the empty one left for Meanie – if he came.

The meeting began – and no Meanie was there. Cheery got up and made a splendid little speech about birthdays, and how they gave everyone a good chance to show people how much you loved them. So what kind of a present should they give Peronel?

And then a loud laugh came through the trees, and Meanie strode into the toadstool ring. "I heard your silly speech!" he cried. "A lot of nonsense. Now just let me tell you what *I* think!"

"Sit down," said Cheery. "It's Jinks's turn to speak next. SIT DOWN, I SAY!"

"Here's *your* seat, Meanie," said Gobo, and pointed to the empty one. Meanie glared round and sat down in a temper – sat down very hard indeed.

Then he suddenly gave such a loud yell that the brownie next to him fell

right off his toadstool in fright.

"Oooooh!" bellowed Meanie, "the pins and needles spell! Ooooh!"

And he leapt up into the air as if he had been stung and ran wailing through the trees, clutching the back of his trousers as he went.

"Good gracious – what's the matter with *him*?" said Whiskers, in surprise.

"Pins and needles. Oooooh!" came Meanie's voice in the distance.

"What does he mean?" said Jinks, in wonder. "Goodness me – you don't mean to say your spell *worked*, Gobo?"

"It seems to have worked very well," said Gobo, grinning. "Anyway – now Meanie's gone – let's get on with the meeting."

They all sat down again, and then Jinks got up to make *his* speech. "I am happy to think that now Meanie has been sent away by Gobo's extraordinary pins and needles spell we can get on with our meeting," he began. Then he stopped suddenly and stared in fright at the one empty seat – the seat that had been Meanie's!

"I say – look! Meanie's seat is walking off!" cried Jinks, in a panic. "*Walking*! Whoever heard of a toadstool *walking*? I'm scared! What with pins and needles spells and walking toadstools . . ."

Gobo began to laugh. He laughed and he laughed. Then he beamed round at everyone. "Didn't I tell you there was more than one way of making spells happen? Well, let me show you how *mine* happened!" And he began to run after the draped seat that was solemnly walking away all by itself. "Hey, pins and needles, stop!"

The seat stopped. Gobo ran up to it and tore off the cloth that was round it.

And will you believe it – it was a prickly *hedgehog*!

The hedgehog promptly curled itself up into a spiky ball, and Gobo laughed. "There you are!" he said to his friends. "My pins and needles spell . . . the hedgehog! I just got him to come here and let me drape a covering over him. Wasn't he a *wonderful* spell? I never *dreamed* that Meanie would sit down quite so hard!"

How everyone roared! Whiskers held his sides and laughed so much that he had to lie down and roll on the grass.

"A pins and needles spell – and it was only Prickles the hedgehog! Oh, to think you've got rid of that awful Meanie by playing a silly trick on him like that!"

"And Meanie *sat* on Prickles – sat down hard in a temper!" cried Cheery. "Oh, I shall never forget this, all my life long. Gobo, you may be no good at *real* spells – but you are *wonderful* at pretend ones!"

Gobo couldn't help feeling pleased. "Now perhaps you won't laugh at me quite so much because I know so little magic," he said. "Well – let's get on with the meeting!"

So there they are, deciding to buy those dancing slippers for Princess Peronel, and wondering who can get the stars to twinkle on the toes – and laughing out loud whenever they think of poor well-pricked Meanie. He'll never come back again, that's certain. He's *much* too scared of clever old Gobo!

The impatient wizard

Once upon a time there was a most impatient wizard. His name was Mr Shout and it was a good one, because whenever he felt impatient he shouted at the top of his voice.

His servant was a scared little brownie called Oh-Dear-Me, with a long beard that was always tripping him up. He was frightened of Mr Shout, and would have left him long ago if it hadn't been for the wizard's dog, Thunder.

Thunder had a growl so exactly like a roll of thunder that there really was no better name for him. He could *look* as black as thunder too and Oh-Dear-Me, the brownie, was even more scared of him than he was of Mr Shout. But he knew that if he ran away Thunder would most certainly catch him.

"Where are you, Oh-Dear-Me!" shouted the wizard from morning to night. "Fetch me a mushroom grown in the light of the moon. I want to make a spell. And bring me a glass of morning dew. And find a spider's web and some caterpillar hairs. I am doing much magic today!"

So it went on, and little Oh-Dear-Me ran about, panting, trying to keep out of the way of Thunder the dog and bring back everything that Mr Shout wanted. He tripped over his beard so often that Mr Shout threatened to cut it off.

"Oh dear me, don't do that!" begged the brownie, in alarm. "I wouldn't be a brownie if I had no beard. Oh dear me, what a terrible job I've got. Get away, Thunder – don't breathe down my neck like that. I haven't had time to make your bone for you yet."

Mr Shout didn't *buy* bones for Thunder. He had given little Oh-Dear-Me a spell for making a large bone each day. It was a very curious spell, and Oh-Dear-Me was a little bit afraid of it.

He made it each day at tea-time while Thunder the dog sat nearby, growling and watching. Oh-Dear-Me was sure that if he ever made a mistake Thunder would eat him instead of the bone!

"You're really a most unpleasant dog," he told Thunder. "And your master is a most unpleasant wizard. Shout and Thunder – you're a well-matched couple – but I wish I didn't have to work for you both!"

One day everything went wrong. Oh-Dear-Me burnt the bacon at breakfast, and spilt hot coffee over Mr Shout's foot. He backed away hurriedly from the angry wizard and fell over Thunder's tail. Thunder growled so loudly that Oh-Dear-Me locked himself in the larder.

"Come out!" shouted the wizard. "If you don't, I'll blow a spell through the key-hole and turn you into a jam tart on the dish."

"Oh dear me, don't do that, you might offer me to one of your friends at tea-time!" said the scared brownie, and he came out of the larder in a hurry.

He was sent to get some strange things for some new magic – a ladybird with thirteen spots – a toadstool with two heads – one brown whisker from a mouse – two prickles from a hedgehog – and one hundred whiskers from gooseberries growing on a bush in the kitchen garden.

Oh-Dear-Me was so flustered that he made a lot of mistakes. He brought back a toadstool with two stalks instead of two heads; he found a ladybird with eleven spots, but he counted wrongly and made them thirteen; he brought a yellow mouse-whisker instead of a brown one; and he picked one hundred prickles from the gooseberry bush, instead of one hundred little whiskery hairs from the gooseberries – and he asked the hedgehog for two of his whiskers instead of two prickles.

He hurried back with everything and found the wizard drawing his usual chalk circle in which to do his magic.

"You're late – I've been waiting a long time for you!" shouted the wizard. "Now then – empty all those things into my pot – and *HURRY!*" Poor Oh-Dear-Me shook everything into the steaming pot and the wizard stepped into the circle of chalk and stirred them all together.

"What are you making today, O Master?" asked Oh-Dear-Me, anxiously. "Not a dragon again, I hope? I really do not like dragons prancing round the place. The last one kept sniffing at me as if I were a biscuit or something."

"Be quiet!" bellowed Mr Shout. "I'm

making a new spell, but I shan't tell
you what it is."

Oh-Dear-Me stood outside the circle,
trembling. Once a thunderstorm had
come out of the pot. Suppose another
came? Would he have time to hide
under the table?

BANG! BONG! BANG!

Green smoke billowed out of the pot,
and loud explosions shook it. The wizard

peered in, surprised. This wasn't at all how the spell should behave. A spire of green smoke billowed into his face, and he stepped back in alarm.

Oh-Dear-Me gave a shriek. "Master, you've gone green! Your face is as green as grass in the springtime! Oh dear me, whatever's happened? You do look funny. Ha-hah-ha, ho!"

Mr Shout took hold of Oh-Dear-Me and shook him so hard that he rattled. Then he set him down with a bump.

"You gave me the wrong *things*! The spell wasn't right. How *dare* you? I'll turn you into a candle-flame and then I'll blow you out – puff!"

"Oh no, Master!" said poor Oh-Dear-Me, stopping his laughter at once. "Oh please no!"

"Yes, that's what I'll do," said Mr Shout. His dog, Thunder, suddenly barked loudly. Mr Shout turned to him.

"Oh, I forgot that it's your tea-time

and you want your bone. Well, Oh-Dear-Me shall make it for you as usual – and after that – puff! He'll be blown out!"

Oh-Dear-Me began to tremble. Perhaps if he made the dog a very, very nice bone things would be all right. Perhaps Mr Shout was just frightening him. He began to scurry round.

First he got a basin of cool clear water. Then he emptied a little green spell into it and stirred it twenty times. Then he muttered six very magic words, and took two hairs from the dog's tail and dropped them into the water.

"Hurry up!" said the wizard, impatiently. "Why are you always so slow? You're the silliest brownie I've ever known. HURRY UP! I'm getting my biggest puff ready for you."

"It's ready, it's ready!" said Oh-Dear-Me, and picked up the basin. Now all he had to do was to pour it inside the magic circle of chalk and it would turn into a big bone . . .

He ran to the circle – but alas, he tripped over his long beard and fell. The basin shot up into the air – and the magic water spilt all over the wizard.

"Oh dear me – what have I done now?" said the poor little brownie sitting on the floor. "Goodness me – where's Mr Shout?"

The wizard was gone. Not a sign of him was to be seen. But on his chair, where he had been sitting, was a most enormous bone. Oh-Dear-Me stared at it in horror.

"Oh my goodness! Oh dear me! What have I done? The magic water must have gone all over the wizard – and he's been changed into that bone. I must get the bone and change it quickly back into the wizard. Dear, dear – where's the changeback spell? How angry he will be! Oh dear, dear, dear me!"

He reached for the bone – but

somebody got it before him. Thunder the dog snapped at it and held it in his mouth. He growled as if to say, "This is *my* bone! Hands off my bone! I'll bite you if you touch it!"

"Don't crunch it – it's your master!" cried Oh-Dear-Me. "Oh, I must go and get help. Poor Mr Shout!"

He ran into the village to get help – but nobody would go back to Mr Shout's house with Oh-Dear-Me. They laughed loudly.

"What a wonderful thing to happen! He's turned into a bone, and nobody will ever be able to get it away from his horrid dog. Don't interfere, Oh-Dear-Me, or you'll get your head bitten off. It's a very fine punishment for that horrid Mr Shout!"

So it was. His dog won't eat the bone, but he won't let anyone else have it either. Well, you can only say one thing about that, and it's what the little brownie says all day long, OH – DEAR – ME!

The magic pinny-minny flower

Too-Thin the magician was making a new spell. He had nearly everything he wanted for it – a bowl of moonlight, a skein of spider's thread, six golden dewdrops, two hairs from a rabbit's tail, and many other things – but there was still one thing he hadn't got.

"I must have a blue pinny-minny flower," said Too-Thin. "That's the only thing I want – a pinny-minny flower. Now I wonder where I can get one."

He went out into his garden to think about it. He walked round and round, up and down the paths, and thought hard. The beds were full of spring daffodils, but Too-Thin didn't notice them. A freckled thrush was singing a new song in the almond tree, but Too-Thin didn't hear it. He didn't even know it was springtime, for he didn't care about things like that.

He frowned and thought harder than ever. He really *must* have a blue pinny-minny flower, but where to get one he couldn't think.

"I must pin a notice outside my gate, and offer a reward to anyone who can bring me what I want," said the magician at last. So he wrote out a notice and pinned it on his gate. This is what it said:

"Six sacks of gold will be given to anyone who brings a blue pinny-minny flower to Too-Thin the magician."

Then Too-Thin went indoors and began to stir the dewdrops in the bowl of moonlight.

Now many people passed by Too-

Thin's gate and read the notice. Nobody knew where to get a blue pinny-minny flower at all. Many of them wrote to witches they knew, and to goblins who lived in mountain caves, asking if they could find a blue pinny-minny flower – but no one could.

One day Higgledy, a tiny cobbler pixie, passed by. He was very poor and lived in a tumble-down cottage with no garden. He often used to peep over the wall that ran round Too-Thin's garden and look at the rows of daffodils there. He wished he could have a garden like it and grow snowdrops, crocuses and daffodils, and roses in the summer-time.

Higgledy read the notice, and then his eyes opened in surprise.

"Surely Too-Thin does not mean this," he said. He climbed up to the top of the wall and sat there, looking into the magician's garden. He looked over the doorway of the house, for he had often seen a tiny plant growing in the stones of the pathway there.

The plant was still there, and Higgledy stared in astonishment.

"Why, there's the pinny-minny plant still growing outside the magician's own door," he said to himself. "I've often seen it when I've looked over the wall. Can it be that the magician doesn't know it's there?"

He jumped over the wall and ran to the door. Yes, it was a pinny-minny plant right enough. Just as he was thinking of knocking at the door and telling the magician, Too-Thin came out, looking rather cross, for he was in a bad temper.

"Now then, now then," he said. "What do you want? Have you come about the eggs?"

"No," said Higgledy, "I'm not the egg-man. I've come about the pinny-minny plant."

"Where is it?" cried the magician. "Have you brought it with you?"

"No," said Higgledy, "you see –"

"Oh, you stupid creature!" cried Too-Thin. "Go and get it at once. Is it in someone's garden? Well, go and pick it! You can pay them for it with the gold I shall give you in return."

Higgledy laughed. He suddenly bent down and picked a blue pinny-minny flower from the plant by his foot. Then he waved it in the magician's face.

"Here it is!" he cried. "You passed it every day when you walked into the garden and never saw it! Oh, Too-Thin, you may be clever at spells, but you are very stupid at other things! Why don't you use your eyes?"

Too-Thin stared in amazement. Why, here was the very flower he had wanted for so long! And to think it grew in his very own garden and he hadn't see it! He went very red as he took it from Higgledy.

"You shall have the six sacks of gold," he said, "even though the plant grew in my own garden. But you must promise not to tell anyone where you found it, for I don't want to be laughed at."

"I promise," said Higgledy. Then the magician sent him to fetch a barrow in which he could wheel home his gold, and whilst Higgledy was gone Too-Thin looked round his garden and saw it for the first time.

"I really must use my eyes more!" he said. "Why, those daffodils are beautiful! And listen to that thrush! Whatever is the use of being a clever magician if I forget to look at daffodils? Well, well, Higgledy has earned his gold, for he has opened my eyes for me!"

Higgledy was so pleased with his good fortune. He bought a beautiful little cottage with a garden and married a nice little wife. And what do you think he called his new cottage? Why, Pinny-Minny Cottage! So if ever you come across it you'll know who lives there!

The enchanted umbrella

O ne day, when Kathleen and Morris had gone to look for blackberries in Cuckoo Wood, they had a strange adventure. It all began because of the rain.

The sun had been shining out of a blue sky when they started out, but when they were deep in the heart of the wood, picking great big blackberries, the sky clouded over.

"Isn't it getting dark?" said Kathleen, looking up at the black sky between the trees. "I'm afraid it's going to pour with rain!"

Just as she spoke the rain came – and how it poured! The children huddled under a thick tree and watched in dismay.

"We haven't got our macs with us," said Morris, "nor even an umbrella! We ought to have brought our raincoats, just in case. Now we shall get soaked!"

They stood under the tree, gazing at the pouring rain. The tree dripped and dripped; everywhere was as wet as could be.

Then suddenly Kathleen stared at something in astonishment, and pointed. "Look!" she cried. "What's that against the tree over there? Is it an umbrella? No, surely it can't be!"

Morris looked, but he couldn't see the umbrella. Kathleen suddenly darted out from beneath the tree to fetch it.

"I don't know who it belongs to," she cried, "but we'll use it to shelter us until the rain has stopped. It looks a lovely big one."

Morris stood under the tree and watched Kathleen run to an oak tree not far off – and there, sure enough, leaning against the trunk was a bright green umbrella with red spots on it! Kathleen ran to it, picked it up and opened it. It was very large indeed, big enough for three or four people to get underneath.

And then a very strange thing happened. Just as Kathleen began to run back to Morris with the green umbrella, she stopped and looked puzzled.

"What's the matter?" called Morris.

"The umbrella is pulling at my hand," said Kathleen – and, as Morris watched, he could quite plainly see that the umbrella was pulling hard at Kathleen. Then he knew that it was magic, and he shouted to Kathleen.

"Let it go! It's enchanted! Let it go, Kathleen!"

"I can't, I can't!" shouted poor Kathleen in a fright. "The handle has taken hold of my hand and it's pulling me along!"

Kathleen was certainly being pulled along, away from Morris. He started to run over to her, but as soon as the umbrella heard him it pulled at Kathleen's hand all the more strongly, and off she went with it, running at top speed between the trees! The umbrella was very clever at dodging the branches, and although Morris ran as hard as he could through the rain, he couldn't catch it.

Soon he had lost sight of it, and he stopped in dismay. Now what was he to do? He *must* find Kathleen somehow! He couldn't let a strange umbrella go off with her like that. He looked round him. He was in another part of the wood, where he had never been before.

"Now I'm lost!" he said. "Oh, goodness, what a dreadful morning!"

Soon he spied a small cottage set under a great oak tree. "I'll go there and ask my way," he thought. He was just about to walk towards the cottage when he heard the sound of someone running through the wood, and to his great surprise he saw a small gnome, with long pointed ears and a long nose. Morris had never seen any of the little people before, though he knew they lived in Cuckoo Wood, and he stared in astonishment.

The gnome was crying loudly, and tears dripped off his nose like raindrops. He ran up the path and banged on the door of the little cottage. Someone opened it, and the gnome began to talk loudly.

"I stood your umbrella by the old oak tree whilst I went to call on my mother!" he wept. "I was only gone a minute and when I came back it had disappeared! Yes, it was quite gone. Oh, dear, I'm so sorry! It was so kind of you to lend it to me, and now I've lost it! Where do you suppose it has gone?"

"Hie, hie!" shouted Morris, running to the cottage in excitement. "I can tell you about that umbrella!"

He ran up the pathway to the little door, hoping that the gnome would help him to get Kathleen back safely. The little gnome stared at him in surprise. At the door stood a brownie with a long beard.

"Come in, both of you," he said. "It's still raining. There's no need to get wet!"

Morris went inside. It was a strange little place, dark and full of furniture. He soon told the gnome what had happened when Kathleen had found the umbrella, and the little man's face became longer and longer as he listened.

"My goodness!" he said sadly. "Who would have thought the umbrella would behave like that?"

"Well, it's an enchanted one, you know," said the brownie. "It used to belong to Dame Twiddle-pins, who lives on the top of Sugar Hill – I expect it's gone back to her!"

"But what about Kathleen?" asked Morris, in dismay.

"Oh, she's gone too," said the brownie. "That used to be an old trick of that umbrella's, when it was young – taking people off to Dame Twiddle-pins. She was half a witch in those days and lived in a great shining palace. She was always wanting people to help her with her spells, so she used to let her umbrella fetch them for her."

"Poor Kathleen!" said Morris. "Whatever shall I do? Which way is it to Sugar Hill?"

"Good gracious, you're not thinking of going to Dame Twiddle-pins, are you?" said the brownie.

"Of course I am," said Morris. "I must rescue Kathleen somehow."

"I'll come with you," said the gnome. "You would never be able to find the way by yourself."

"Oh, thank you," said Morris, gratefully. "We'd better start now. It's stopped raining."

The brownie went to the door and saw them off. The gnome took Morris through the trees until he came to a very tall one.

"We climb up this," he said. Morris looked at it. He liked climbing trees, but this one was very difficult. It was soaked with rain and was green and slippery.

The gnome swung himself up on a branch and began to climb – but in a second he was down again, his nice red suit all covered in green.

"We'll have to go up inside," he said. "I'll just knock and see if it's convenient."

To Morris's surprise he knocked on the tree with a little wooden knocker that looked like a knob of bark. A small door opened in the trunk and an old lady looked out.

"What do you want?" she asked. "If you're selling scissors, I don't want any today."

"We're not selling anything," said the gnome, politely. "We just want to know if you'd mind us using your stairs inside the tree today. It's so slippery outside."

"All right," said the old woman. "But see that you wipe your feet!"

They stepped inside the big tree and wiped their feet carefully on the mat. Morris was astonished to see that he was in a hall. An open door looked into a cosy kitchen with a bright fire. Two other doors were shut. A spiral stairway was in the middle of the tree, and the gnome led the way up this.

"This tree belongs to old Mrs Acorn," he said. "She lets all the rooms in it to lodgers. We shall pass their doors as we go up."

Morris was more and more astonished. They went up the staircase, and as they passed each landing he looked at the doors. Some had brass plates on them, with printed names. 'Frisky Squirrel' was on one plate. 'Mister Fiddle-sticks' on another. Morris wondered what he could be like.

As they passed one door it opened

and a small pixie looked out. "Oh," she said in disappointment, "I thought you were the washing coming." Before Morris could say anything she had shut the door.

They went up and up, passing many rooms on the way. At last the tree narrowed until there was only room for the stairway. Then that ended in a small platform, and Morris and the gnome came out at the very top of the tree.

Morris stepped on to the platform and looked round. He was right at the very top of the wood! The tree they had climbed was higher than any other, and Morris could see far down below him the green, waving tops of the other trees.

"Where do we go now?" he asked.

"We must wait for the cloud bus," said the gnome, picking acorns off the top of the tree, and throwing them down through the branches. Morris felt excited. The cloud bus! Whatever could that be like? He watched for it, and very soon saw a strange-looking carriage bumping along over the clouds. It seemed to be made of clouds itself, and was painted all the colours of the rainbow. It came rolling to the top of the tree, and stopped at the platform. Its wheels were set with misty wings, and it was these that sent it along.

"Get in," said the gnome. Morris stepped in half-frightened, for really, the bus didn't look strong enough to hold him. But it was! He sat down on a seat and looked round. There were only two other passengers, a man in a pointed hat who looked like a wizard, and a very stiff-looking rabbit dressed in a black coat and a high collar, with a shiny top hat on his head. His ears stuck out at each side and made Morris want to laugh, but the rabbit looked so solemn that he didn't like to.

The conductor came to give them tickets. The gnome gave him two pennies, which, to Morris's surprise, were green instead of brown, and asked for Sugar Hill.

"Sorry," said the conductor, who was a small brownie with his beard tucked neatly into his belt. "We don't go there, you know. The nearest we go is Sleepy Town."

"Well, we'll go there, then," said the gnome. "I don't *want* to," he said to Morris, "because it's a dreadful place to get out of. It's so difficult to find anyone who will tell you the way."

The bus went on through the air, the little wings on the wheels flying and making them go round. The next stop was Tip-up Corner. Morris thought it a very good name for whatever place it was, for the bus tipped up and he and the other two passengers all went sliding to the front. The rabbit's top hat came off and he was very much upset. He went after it and fell right out of the bus. Morris saw him tumbling down through the air.

"He's all right," said the conductor. "He nearly always gets out like that. Sleepy Town's the next stop. I'll put you down in the market-place."

The bus went on to Sleepy Town. It flew downwards for a change and Morris saw that it was on the ground again, its wheels still moving by means of the little wings. Soon it came to a quiet, sleepy-looking village and stopped in the market-place.

"Here you are," said the conductor. "Sleepy Town!"

They got out and looked round. There were a few stalls in the market, but under the big umbrellas that protected their goods from the sun, the people of Sleepy Town sat, fast asleep. They were round, fat little people, with button noses and shiny cheeks. Morris felt sleepy himself when he looked at them. He yawned loudly. The gnome looked at him in alarm.

"I say, don't do that!" he said. "If you once go to sleep here, you might not wake up for months."

"Good gracious!" said Morris, alarmed. "I'll be careful, then."

"The thing is – which way do we go to Sugar Hill?" said the gnome. "If only we could find someone to ask! They are all sound asleep!"

"Wake them then!" said Morris. He went up to a small fat boy who sat fast asleep against a wall, his mouth wide open. Morris shook him. Then he shook him again. All that happened was that the boy shut his mouth, and began to snore.

"It's no good," said the gnome, watching. "You never *can* wake anyone up in Sleepy Town. If we could find the fire-bell we might be able to. That's about the only thing they listen to!"

"Come on, then, let's find it," said Morris. So they looked up and down the crooked little streets – and at last Morris found the fire-station! Inside was a bright and shining fire-engine – and by it, hanging on the wall, was a great fire-bell.

"Good!" cried Morris. He ran to it, took it down and rang it. Goodness, what a clanging it made!

The gnome almost jumped out of his skin – and then, in the same minute he cried, "Look out! The fire-engine is moving!"

Morris looked round and saw the fire-engine rushing towards him all by itself. He had no time to get out of the way, so he quickly jumped up on the front of it with his bell. The gnome jumped on too, and off they both went on the swift fire-engine!

But the streets were no longer sleepy. Everyone had awakened as if by magic! They jumped up, they came rushing out of the houses, they shouted loudly. When they saw the fire-engine they were more excited than ever.

"Where's the fire?" they called, to the gnome and Morris. This was awkward. There was no fire, of course. Morris thought it was better not to answer that question. Instead he asked another.

"Which is the way to Sugar Hill?"

"Oh, is that where the fire is?" shouted the fat little people. "Down to the right, across the river, and you'll see Sugar Hill in the distance. Hurry there and we'll follow and help you to put the fire out!"

The gnome began to laugh when he saw the round Sleepy Town folk jumping on bicycles, and getting into carts and cars to find out where the fire was. "We've woken them up all right," he said. "How do you steer this fire-engine? We must make it go the right way."

It didn't seem to need any steering at all. It rushed to the right, round a corner, and thundered towards a river that shone in the distance. It rolled over a wide bridge, and then Morris and the gnome saw, glittering in the distance, a curious hill, as white as snow. On the top stood a small house which looked as if it might topple over at any moment!

"There's Sugar Hill!" said the gnome, pleased.

On went the fire-engine, and as it came near Sugar Hill Morris saw that it was unwinding long hoses.

"Look!" he said to the gnome. "The engine really thinks there's a fire!"

"And look behind you!" said the gnome. "The whole of Sleepy Town is coming after us!"

So it was! Hundreds of the little fat people were coming along in crowds, eager to see where the fire was. Morris began to wonder what they would say when they knew there was no fire!

The engine stopped at the foot of the white sugary hill. Morris and the gnome jumped off. They began to climb the hill, slipping backwards

every now and then in the snow-
like sugar. When they reached the
top they looked at the strange house
that rested there. It really looked as
though a good strong push would send
it down to the bottom of the hill on
the other side!

Outside the door stood the enchanted
umbrella, green, with red spots! Morris
gave a shout when he saw it, and so
did the gnome. So Kathleen was here
after all! Good!

Morris was going to knock at the
door when the gnome stopped him.
"Don't do that," he whispered. "If
old Dame Twiddle-pins comes she'll
be angry to see that we've brought
half Sleepy Town with us. Peep in
at the window."

So Morris crept to the window and
peeped inside the house. The first
thing he saw was Kathleen sitting
in a corner, crying. She was trying
to sew a great checked duster with
a coarse, blunt needle, and it was

dreadfully hard work. The tears fell on the duster, and Morris felt very sorry for Kathleen. Then he saw Dame Twiddle-pins, nodding, half-asleep, in a rocking-chair. If only he could make Kathleen see him!

He tapped gently on the window, and then bobbed down in case the old woman should look up and see him. Then he heard a deep voice speaking, the voice of Dame Twiddle-pins.

"Go to the window, girl, and look out. It sounds as if a bird is tapping at the pane. It may be my pigeon. Let it in."

Kathleen went to the window and opened it. As soon as she leaned out she saw Morris crouching underneath. He beckoned to her to jump out of the window, and at once she did so, delighted to see her brother. He dragged her down to him and then they crept round to the other side of the house, where the gnome was.

"Oh, Morris!" said Kathleen, happily. "I knew you'd rescue me! That horrid old woman has made me do all sorts of nasty, hard jobs for her, ever since that umbrella brought me here, and she wouldn't let me go home."

Just then there was an angry shout from inside the house.

"Girl! Where are you? Come back at once or I'll come and fetch you."

Morris, the gnome and Kathleen crouched together on the other side of the house. The old woman ran to the door and stood there, looking for Kathleen – and at that very moment the fire-engine filled its long hose with water, held it up like an elephant's trunk and squirted a great jet all over Dame Twiddle-pins! She gave a loud scream of surprise and fright and fell backwards into the kitchen, soaked through. She went to the open window, shouting with rage, and the engine squirted water through that too. Then up the hill came climbing all the little fat people of Sleepy Town, carrying buckets of water, and what a time they had!

They flung their water everywhere, and soon the inside of the house was dripping wet. Dame Twiddle-pins was quite beside herself with rage and amazement, for she couldn't imagine what everyone was doing – and at last so fierce and angry was she that the Sleepy Town people stopped and listened to her.

"How dare you, how dare you!" shouted the old woman, shaking her stick at them.

"We came to put out the fire," said one of the Sleepy Town people.

"I didn't have a fire!" shouted Dame Twiddle-pins.

"But a boy rang the fire-bell and started the fire-engine off here," said another.

"Oh, that's someone come to get the girl I had here then," said Dame Twiddle-pins, in a rage. "Well, find them. They must be somewhere about. The hill's too steep to get down at the back and we should have seen anyone climbing down the front!"

Morris, Kathleen and the gnome wondered whatever they were going to do. They were still hiding at the back of the house. The gnome suddenly stood up and grinned. "I've thought of something!" he said. "Wait here for me!"

He slipped round the side of the house to the front door. Everyone was most astonished to see him, and no one tried to capture him at all. They just stood with their mouths and eyes wide open in surprise!

The gnome caught up the green umbrella, dashed round the house with it and opened it. He hooked it on to his belt, held out a hand to each of the two children, and shouted suddenly in a very loud voice, "Home, Umbrella!"

The umbrella immediately tugged hard at the gnome's belt and began to take them down the hill at the back. It was very steep, but with the help of the umbrella and the gnome, the children managed all right. Everyone came running round to the back of the house, Dame Twiddle-pins too, and how they shouted to see the three escaping.

"You woke us up, you bad boy!" cried one of the Sleepy Town people, shaking his fist.

"You took our fire-engine," roared another.

"You've spoilt my house!" screamed Dame Twiddle-pins.

"Goodbye, goodbye, see you another time!" called the gnome, cheekily, as they all reached the bottom of the hill. The umbrella took them swiftly along. It seemed to know its way marvellously well. In less than ten minutes it was back in Cuckoo Wood, dodging between the still-wet trees in a very clever manner.

It stopped outside the brownie's house and the gnome unhooked it from his

belt. The brownie opened his door and looked out. The umbrella walked into his kitchen and put itself into a small umbrella-stand there. It really was a marvellous umbrella!

"So you're safely back!" said the brownie. "Well, come in and have a cup of cocoa. I've got some made for you. Then you, Gnome, can take the children home."

So they all went in and drank hot, sweet cocoa, and told the brownie about their strange adventures. When he heard about the people throwing water over Dame Twiddle-pins he laughed till he cried.

"That will serve her right!" he said, wiping his eyes. "She's a hard, mean old creature, and that will teach her a lesson! Oh, dear, oh, dear, how I wish I'd been there!"

"I think it's time we went home," said Morris, at last. So they said goodbye to the brownie, promised to go and see him again, and went with the gnome, who saw them safely to the edge of the wood. Then off they ran home, longing to tell their mother all that had happened.

But she thought that they had made it all up – so tomorrow they are going to take her to the brownie's house in the wood, and show her that strange and surprising thing – the brownie's enchanted umbrella!

The wizard and
the Rubdubs

Once upon a time little Prince Philomel was on his travels round Fairyland, when he suddenly saw a curious sight. Coming towards him was a crowd of little people, all looking very miserable. None of them wore hats, and they all had heads as bald as eggs.

One of them was dressed much more grandly than the others and Philomel spoke to him.

"Who are you, and what's the matter with you all?" he asked.

"We are the Rubdubs," answered the little man, with tears trickling down his cheeks. "I am the King of the Rubdubs, and my palace isn't very far away. A great misfortune has befallen us, as you can see."

"Tell me about it," said Philomel.

"Well, we were all out walking this morning," began the little King, "and we met a very kind-looking wizard. He invited us into his cottage, and offered us some lovely coloured sweets out of a tin. We each took one, and no sooner had we swallowed it than what do you think happened?"

"What?" asked Philomel.

"Why, every hair on our heads fell out!" wept the little King, and all the Rubdubs wept too, so that a big puddle began to form on the path.

"Well, but didn't you tell the wizard to put your hair back for you at once?" asked Philomel in surprise.

"Of *course* we did!" said the King. "But all he said was – 'Pay me a hundred gold crowns and I will show you how to get your hair back.' Well I haven't got even fifty gold crowns,

because it is expensive to be a King nowadays, and besides, I spent all my money on my palace, which is a very beautiful one. So we had to come away bald!"

He cried big tears again, and Philomel wished he had wellingtons on.

"Never mind," he said. "I'll put things right for you. I'll go straight to that rogue of a wizard now."

"Oh, be careful, be careful," begged the Rubdub King. "You'll come back bald or something, really you will! He's a wicked creature, that wizard!"

But Philomel only laughed. He knew what the Rubdubs didn't know – and that was that no spell of any sort could harm him, for a witch had once rubbed him with fresh elderflower under the new moon, and that kept all harm from him.

He went along to where the Rubdubs had told him the wizard lived. Sure enough, he soon saw a cottage. Someone was peering from the window and, as soon as Philomel drew near, the wizard came out of the front door.

"A nice morning, a very nice morning," he said to Philomel, smiling very broadly.

"It is," said Philomel. "What a lovely place this is to live in! How lucky you are to have your cottage in this wood!"

"Indeed I am," said the wizard. "But won't you come in for a moment and see it? I have many curious things inside which I'm sure you'd like to see."

"Thank you," said Philomel, and he followed the grinning wizard inside the hut.

"Sit down, sit down," said the wizard. He went to a cupboard and opened it. He took out a large tin and went across to Philomel.

"Have a sweet?" he asked. "They're most delicious. I bought them from an old witch yesterday. They make you feel lovely."

"Thank you very much," said Philomel, knowing quite well that the sweets were the same as those that had made all the little Rubdubs bald. He popped it into his mouth and crunched it. It certainly tasted delicious. The wizard watched him closely, and when Philomel's hair did not fall off, he looked very puzzled.

Then Philomel did a bit of pretending. He jumped up from his chair and clapped his hands with joy.

"Oh!" he cried. "That was a magic sweet! Oh! I am full of the most powerful magic now! I know things I never knew before! I can read the stars! I can hear the grass growing! I know all the languages in the world!"

"What!" cried the wizard. "Can you really? I must have given you the wrong sweet!"

"Oh, give me more, give me more!" cried Philomel, enjoying himself very much. He snatched four or five from the tin and crunched them up loudly.

Then he danced round the room.

"I know more magic than anyone else in the world! The sweets are telling me all the secrets of Fairyland! I am getting more powerful every minute! Oh, give me more of those wonderful sweets!"

He snatched at the tin again, but the wizard pushed him away.

"*No!*" he said. "I shall eat the rest myself! I'm not going to have you taking all the magic like this. I'd no idea I'd got such wonderful sweets. All the top ones were quite different. They simply made people bald!"

He greedily filled his mouth full of the sweets and crunched them up. Then he waited to feel the magic coming but nothing happened – but wait a minute – yes, something *was* happening! What was this tumbling down on the floor? Oh my, oh my, it was the wizard's fine, thick hair!

"I've eaten the wrong sweets! Oh, oh! I'm bald like the Rubdubs!" he cried. "Oh, what a dreadful thing, for I'm going out to tea this afternoon, and how can I go bald? Oh, I must quickly find a spell to put it right again."

Philomel pretended to be very sorry for him. He helped him to look through all his magic books until he had found how to get his hair back again.

"I must make a mixture of new honey, six dewdrops, the scent of a violet, some silk from a spider's web, some bottled moonlight and stir it all up with an owl's feather," said the wizard in a trembling voice. "Oh dear, oh dear! Well, it's easy enough to get the first four things, but I haven't very much bottled moonlight left, I'm afraid."

He took down a bottle and shook it.

"Only just enough," he said. He quickly made the mixture, poured in the silver moonlight, and stirred it all up with an owl's feather.

"Now if you'll help me," he said to Philomel, "I shall soon be all right

again, with all my hair back safely.
I must kneel down in a chalk circle,
close my eyes and count fifty. Then
you must pour the mixture over my
head, and all my hair will grow again
as thick and as long as before."

Philomel took the bottle with the
mixture in, and waited until the wizard
was kneeling down with his eyes closed,
counting fifty. Then, very quietly,
Philomel stole out of the door, and
ran back to the Rubdubs as fast as
he could.

"Quick, quick!" he said. "Kneel down,
shut your eyes and count fifty. I'm just
going to draw a chalk circle round you,
and then pour this magic stuff over
your heads!"

In a second all the Rubdubs were
on their knees, counting. When they
came to fifty, Philomel poured a little
of the moonlight mixture on each of
their little bald heads, and sure enough
the hair sprouted again and grew long
and thick and curly! How delighted the

Rubdubs were, and how they crowded round Philomel and begged him to come and stay at their palace.

Suddenly there came a noise like an angry bull, and the wizard burst upon them, his eyes flashing wildly.

"You've taken my mixture!" he cried. "I waited and waited for you to pour it, and you were gone! Oh, you've used it all on those wretched little Rubdubs! Oh, you thief, you robber!"

Philomel laughed.

"You're the thief and the robber!" he said. "You took away the Rubdubs' hair, and I gave it back to them. Here you are, catch! There's your precious bottle back, but it's empty!"

The wizard caught it and hurried away. He managed to squeeze two drops from it and rubbed them on his bald head, but as only four long hairs grew, he looked funnier than ever.

Still, as Philomel said, it really *did* serve him right!

The spelling spell

Once Mr Stamp-About went through Dimity Wood in a great rage. He stamped as he went and muttered to himself, and he even shook his fist in the air.

"I'll pay old Snorty back for not giving me what he owes me! How am I to pay *my* bills if he doesn't pay his? How dare he say that the apples I sold him were bad, and not worth a penny! How *dare* he not pay me for them!"

The rabbits ran away from his stamping feet, and the squirrels bounded up into the trees. The robin followed him, flying from tree to tree in wonder. What was the matter now with noisy old Stamp-About?

Stamp-About didn't notice that he had taken the wrong path in the wood. He went on and on, and then suddenly found that the path was getting very narrow. He stopped and looked round.

"I've taken the wrong path! All because of Snorty! I am so angry with him that I don't even see the way I am walking!"

He stood there a few moments, wondering what to do. "Perhaps there's someone nearby who will hear me if I shout, and tell me the right path," he thought. So he gave a loud shout. "Ho there! I want help!"

Nobody answered at all, and the birds all flew away in fright, for Stamp-About had such a tremendous voice! He yelled again. "Ho there! I want help!"

And this time a voice called back to him – a very cross voice indeed.

"Will you be quiet? You're spoiling

my spell!"

Stamp-About could hardly believe his ears. Spoiling someone's spell? Whose? And if the someone was near enough to shout back, why didn't he come to help Stamp-About? "Rude fellow!" thought Stamp-About, angrily. "I'll go and tell him what I think of him!"

So he pushed his way fiercely through the bushes and came to a little clearing, set neatly round with red-spotted toadstools in a ring. In the middle sat a little fellow in a long black cloak that shimmered like moonlight. He had two long feelers on his forehead, just like a butterfly.

In front of him a small fire burnt, and on it was a clear bowl of glass, which, strangely enough, seemed not to mind the flames at all.

"Why didn't you come to help me?" stormed Stamp-About.

"Please go away," said the little fellow, turning round. "Yelling like that in my spell time, I never heard of such a thing! Go and buy yourself a few manners!"

Stamp-About almost exploded with temper. "How dare you," he cried. "Who are you, you – you miserable, uncivil little fellow!"

"I'm Weeny, the little wizard," said the small man. "And I get my living by making spells at this time each day and selling them. And then *you* come blustering along and spoil them all. Just when I was making gold, too! Pah!"

"*Gold*?" said Stamp-About, in quite a different voice. "Good gracious – can you make *gold*?"

"Not exactly," said the little wizard. "But my spells can! I've only to pop the right things into my little glass bowl here, and spell each one as they dissolve – and at the end what do I find? A handful of gold at the bottom of my bowl!"

"*Really*?" said Stamp-About, wishing he hadn't been rude. "Er – I'm sorry I disturbed you. Please start all over again! But why do you have to *spell* each word – why can't you just *say* it?"

"Don't be silly," said the little wizard. "A spell is a spell because it's *spelt*, isn't it? You can't make a spell unless you spell it, can you?"

"I don't know," said Stamp-About, and he came into the toadstool ring, treading on one as he did so.

"Get out!" said the wizard, pointing a long thin finger at him. "Treading on my magic toadstool! Get out! I'll turn you into a worm and call down that robin over there to eat you if you're not careful!"

Stamp-About hurriedly stepped out of the ring of toadstools, being very careful not to break one again.

"Now go away, and let me start my gold spell all over again," commanded the fierce little fellow.

Stamp-About tiptoed away, and hid behind a tree. All right – let the wizard order him about all he liked – he would hide and watch the spell and then *he* would make it too, when he got home! Aha – gold for the making – what a wonderful thing!

He peeped from behind a tree and watched. The wizard took no more notice of him. He had a pile of things to put into the glass bowl – but first he poured into it some water from a little jug.

Then he took a buttercup and shredded its golden petals one by one into the bowl, muttering as he did so. Stamp-About strained his ears, but he couldn't catch what was being said, until he heard the wizard say, "C-U-P."

"Of course – he's only *spelling* the name of the flower!" thought Stamp-About. "Now – what's he putting in this time? Oh – one of the red toadstools. And now he's spelling that. Ho – what an easy spell to make!"

He watched carefully. The little wizard took another buttercup and spelt out its name – then he took a

twig of hawthorn blossom and shook the white petals into the bowl, and then another buttercup.

"He's spelling everything," thought Stamp-About. "Well, who would have thought that *spelling* had anything to do with the making of spells? This is going to be very useful to me! What is he taking now?"

The wizard had picked up the empty shell of a robin's egg and had crushed it up and dropped it into the bubbling water, which was a bright mixture of colours. He muttered as he spelt the name, and then threw in yet another shower of buttercup petals.

Then he danced lightly round the bowl three times and stopped. To Stamp-About's astonishment all the water in the bowl rose up as a cloud of steam – leaving a gleaming handful of gold at the bottom of the bowl!

"Look at that," whispered Stamp-About to himself in glee, as he watched the wizard put the gold into a wallet. "Now I know exactly how to make the spell. I'll go home and do it."

The little wizard took up the bowl, put it into a small bag, and then he stamped out the fire. He disappeared like a shadow through the trees.

"I'll follow him," thought Stamp-About. "He must know the way out of this wood."

So he followed carefully, and soon came to a path he knew. He went one way and the little wizard went the other. Stamp-About was so excited that he went home smiling all over his face – much to the surprise of Snorty, who was leaning over his gate as Stamp-About passed.

"You're in a better temper now, are you?" called Snorty. "Well, perhaps now you'll admit that those apples of yours *were* bad – and that I don't owe you for them after all!"

"I don't need a penny from you, Snorty, not a penny!" said Stamp-About. "I shall soon be rich. I shall pay all the bills I owe – and you'll come borrowing from *me*, you see if you don't!"

Well, this was very astonishing news to Snorty, who soon spread it about that Stamp-About was going to be rich.

"How?" asked his friends. "What's he going to do? Let's go round and ask him."

When they came to Stamp-About's house he was out in his garden. He had made a small fire in the middle of the lawn, and on it he had placed a little glass bowl – the one in which his goldfish once used to swim.

"Look at that," said Snorty in amazement. "What's he doing? See – he's got a pile of queer things beside him – buttercups – a red toadstool – and what's that – the shell of an egg? And look, there's a spray of hawthorn blossom too, off the may hedge."

Stamp-About saw everyone watching and was very pleased to show off. He did exactly as he had seen the little wizard do – first he threw in the buttercup petals, shredding them off the flower head one by one. As he did so, he spelt the name out loud in a high chanting voice.

"B-u-t-e-r-c-u-p!"

Then he took up the red toadstool and put that into the bowl of water too. Again he chanted out loud, spelling the name clearly.

"R-e-d t-o-a-d-s-t-o-o-l!"

Then he shredded buttercup petals again and spelt the name as before, and then took the hawthorn blossom.

"H-o-r-t-h-o-r-n!"

And in went the white may petals as he shook the twig over the bowl! Aha – the water was changing colour now. Soon the handful of gold would come!

In went more buttercup petals and the name was spelt: "B-u-t-e-r-c-u-p!"

Then he dropped in the broken shell of a robin's egg. As he crumpled up the shell and it fell into the water Stamp-About spelt out the name in a loud voice. "R-o-b-b-i-n's e-g-g!"

And last of all another shower of golden buttercup petals went into the bubbling water.

Eagerly Stamp-About leaned over it. Now for the gold! First the water would disappear in a cloud of steam

– and then he would see the handful of gold at the bottom of the bowl!

But wait – first he must dance three times round the bowl!

Everyone crept forward to see what was about to happen. A cloud of steam shot high into the air and the water in the bowl disappeared. Then the bowl itself exploded with such a bang that everyone fell over backwards.

Stamp-About sat down very suddenly indeed, scared almost out of his wits. Then he looked eagerly at the fire – had the gold been scattered about all round it?

No – there wasn't a single piece of gold. The fire had gone out when the bowl exploded, and now only one thing lay there – a large book!

"What's happened?" shouted Stamp-About in a rage. "The spell's gone wrong! It should have made gold, not a stupid book. What book is it?"

He took it up and opened it – then he looked up in astonishment and everyone crowded round to see what it was.

"It's a *dictionary*!" said Snorty, and gave a huge guffaw. "Ha ha, ho ho, I'm not surprised."

"But – why did the spell go wrong?" cried Stamp-About, and dashed the book to the ground. "I don't want a *dictionary*!"

"Yes, you do!" chuckled Snorty. "The spell went wrong because your *spelling* went wrong! Spells have to be spelled correctly! That's why all you've got is a dictionary – to help you to spell. Oh, what a joke! Can you spell 'rotten apples', Stamp-About? Oh, what a comical thing! He tried to make a spell – but he couldn't even *spell*!"

It was quite true. The spell couldn't work unless everything was spelled out correctly – and Stamp-About had conjured up something he needed as much as gold: a dictionary. Poor old Stamp-About, he hasn't paid his bills *yet*!

Buttercup magic

Now, one morning, old Mother Doodah went across the buttercup field with her shopping. She had a very full basket, and on the top of it was a pat of lovely golden butter that she had bought from the butter-woman in the market.

Mother Doodah put her basket down to do up her shoe. She didn't see that the pound of butter had slipped down into the buttercups. She got up again, and went off with her shopping – but the butter lay in the field, as golden as the buttercups.

Who should come along but the four naughty little imps who lived at the bottom of the field in an old hollow

tree. One of them tripped over the butter.

"What's this?" said Higgle.

"Butter!" said Piggle, poking it.

"What a lot!" said Tick, and he tried to pick it up, but it was almost as big as he was.

"We'll take it home," said Tock. "I wonder who dropped it?"

"Mother Doodah, I expect," said Higgle. "She always brings her shopping back across this field."

Not one of them thought of running after Mother Doodah to ask her if she had dropped the butter. Higgle poked his finger right through the paper and into the butter. "Oooh – isn't it lovely!"

He had butter on his finger and he licked it off.

"Don't do that," said Piggle. "It's not your butter!"

" 'Tis!" said Higgle. "I found it. Don't talk to me like that, Piggle, or I shan't let you have even a lick." He poked his finger into the butter, and licked it again.

Tick poked his finger in, too, but Higgle pushed him away. "You can only do that if I say so," he said. "It's *my* butter. I found it."

"You didn't! You only tripped over it!" said Tick. "Mean thing!"

"You're always mean," said Tock, and he gave Higgle a push that sent him almost headfirst into the butter.

"Now then, stop that!" said Higgle, looking very fierce. "I tell you, this is *my butter*, and if any of you behave badly to me you won't get any of it. Not a lick!"

Piggle, Tick and Tock shouted angrily at him, but they didn't dare to touch the butter again. Higgle could be very fierce when he wanted to.

And then a voice came from behind them. "Now, now – what's all this quarrelling? What is the noise about? I was having a nap and you disturbed me!"

The four imps turned round and saw Sly the goblin. Higgle pointed to the butter.

"See that butter? I found it. So it's mine, isn't it? You say it's mine, Sly, and I'll give you a big piece."

"Now, now," said Sly. "We can easily find out whose this butter is. Very easily indeed. I'm quite sure that you don't *all* like butter, do you? Quite a lot of imps never even eat it."

"I like it!" cried Higgle, and the others said the same.

"Well, we'll prove it," said Sly. "I don't expect more than one of you likes butter, and if Higgle found the butter I daresay he's the one that likes it. If I find any one of you others liking it, well, you shall have a share, too."

"But how are you going to find out who likes butter and who doesn't?" said Higgle, impatiently. "I think this is silly. The butter's mine."

" 'Tisn't!" yelled the others. "We *all*

found it. You just happened to trip over it!"

"Be quiet," said Sly, sternly. "I will now show you the old, old way of finding out who likes butter. It was discovered by my great-great-great-grandma about four hundred years ago!"

The imps looked at him in surprise. "Show us," they said.

Sly picked a golden buttercup. "Watch," he said, and he tilted up his chin, and looked up into the sky. "I'm going to hold this buttercup under my chin. If a gold patch comes under my chin, as yellow as butter, that shows I like butter. Will you please look and see if I do?"

The imps crowded near to look. They saw a bright gold patch spreading under the goblin's chin, reflected from the buttercup.

"You like butter, yes, you do. Very, very much!" called the imps. "Now do that to us! See if *we* like butter, too.

And if we all do, we *all* share the butter, don't we?"

"Yes, yes. Don't make such a noise," said Sly. "Now, please do what I say. Sit down in a ring, with your backs to each other. Tilt up your chins, and look straight up at the sky. And sit like that and wait till I come round with the buttercup. I'll hold it under your chins and at the end I'll tell you what I see."

So the four imps did as they were told and sat in a ring, their backs to one another. They tilted up their chins and looked right up into the sky.

They waited, and they waited. Their necks began to feel stiff, but still they waited. What a long time Sly was taking over finding out who liked butter!

At last Higgle couldn't hold up his head any longer. He put his chin down and looked round for Sly. But Sly wasn't there!

"The *butter's* not there, either!" shouted Higgle, and that made the other three imps put their chins down, too, and look round in astonishment.

"Sly's gone – and so has the butter!" cried Higgle. "Oh, the wretch! Oh, the rogue! He didn't mean to find out if we liked butter at all! He just meant to go off with it himself. Why did we quarrel about it? Why didn't we remember that Sly loves butter with his bread?"

"After him! After him!" shouted Tick, and all four imps raced across the field, under the stile and into the next field, where they knew Sly lived.

But they hadn't gone very far into the next field when they heard an angry voice. It was Mother Doodah's. The imps peeped through the long grasses and the tall buttercups.

Mother Doodah was holding Sly by the collar and she was shaking him so hard that the imps could hear his teeth rattling in his head. Shake, shake, shake! Rattle, rattle!

"What do you mean, running off with my butter? *I* saw you, slinking through the grasses with it, you wicked little goblin!" Shake, shake, shake!

"I didn't take it, it was the four imps, *they* found it!" wept Sly. "I was taking it back to you, really I was!"

"Oh, you were, were you – and dipping your finger into it all the way and sucking off the butter!" cried the angry old woman. "Well, if I catch those four imps I'll ask them if what you say is true – and if it is, they'll get a shaking as well as you!" Shake, shake, shake! Rattle, rattle!

The four imps ran off as fast as ever they could. Dear, dear – to think that Sly had been caught by Mother Doodah like that!

"It serves him right," said Higgle, when they were safely in their hollow tree.

"Well – it might have happened to *us*," said Piggle. "I think now we should have run after Mother Doodah and given the butter back to her."

"We certainly should," said Tick, remembering how Mother Doodah had shaken Sly.

"We will another time," said Tock. "Ha, ha! I *shall* laugh at Sly next time I see him."

Poor Sly had been shaken almost to bits, and he had gone to Old Man Jigsaw to be put together properly again, so they didn't see him for a very long time.

The funny thing is, of course, that he was quite right about buttercups showing who likes butter! The little bit of magic in them still works. Hold one under your friend's chin, and see whether the little golden patch shows there, or not.

It's really rather strange, isn't it?

The magic acorn

Sammy was always reading stories about magic. He wished he had a magic wand. He wished he could have three wishes that came true. He wished he could say "Hey presto!" to something and change it into something else!

But he couldn't seem to find any magic anywhere. Once he saw a curious silver stick in somebody's house and he took it out and waved it in the air, hoping it was magic. But it wasn't. It was only the silver stick that the old lady of the house used to help her along.

Another time he read some magic words in a story and he thought perhaps if he said them at midnight he might work a spell – but although he said them hundreds of times, nothing happened at all. It was very disappointing.

Then one day, when he was walking home through the woods, he met an old woman who was picking up acorns and putting them into her basket.

"What are you getting the acorns for?" asked Sammy.

"For my pig," said the old woman, looking at Sammy out of twinkling blue eyes. "My pig loves acorns."

"I suppose you are not a fairy woman or a witch or anything, are you?" asked Sammy, thinking that often the old women that people met in woods used to be fairies.

"I'm afraid I'm not," said the old lady. "I'm so sorry to disappoint you. Why – are you looking for somebody like that?"

"I'm always looking for magic," said Sammy. "But I never find any. You know, I'd love someone to say to me, 'Here is a green powder – shake it

over a cat and it will change to a tiger' – or something like that."

"Well – I can't say that I would like to change my cat into a tiger," said the old lady. "But, you know, there is lots of magic about if you know the right place to look for it, little boy."

"Tell me some," said Sammy.

"I found a caterpillar in the spring," said the old lady, "and after it had eaten well, it took off its skin and wove itself a cocoon to sleep in. But when it woke up – hey presto! some magic had been at work – and it had changed into a marvellous moth, all red and white and black!"

"Where did it get its wings from?" asked Sammy. "Caterpillars don't have wings – but moths do."

"I don't know how it got wings," said the old lady. "I tell you, it was magic of some kind. And now look – here is another bit of magic. Take this acorn home with you – there is an oak tree inside it!"

Sammy took the smooth, polished acorn, so nice to hold in his hand. He looked at it and laughed.

"What! An oak tree in a tiny acorn like this!" he said. "I don't believe you! An oak tree is enormous – why, look at the one we are standing under, it stretches almost up to the sky."

"So it does," said the old woman. "Well, take that acorn home, my dear, and plant it in a small acorn-glass. You can buy one for a few pence. Then watch the magic begin. I tell you there is an oak tree in that acorn, no matter what you say!"

Sammy put the acorn in his pocket and ran home. He asked his mother to buy him an acorn-glass, and she did. It was like the bulb-vase that the children grew bulbs in at school, but very, very much smaller. The vase was squeezed in a little at the neck, leaving a place to hold the acorn at the top.

"The old lady who gave me this

acorn said there was an oak tree inside," said Sammy. "Just think! A big oak tree inside this tiny acorn. Well – we'll see."

He filled the acorn-vase with water up to the neck. Then he set the acorn and glass on the window-sill. He forgot all about it for two weeks. Then his mother called him.

"Look!" she said. "Your acorn is putting out a root, Sammy. Would you think there was a root inside that acorn?"

The acorn had quite a long white root! It put it right down into the water. Sammy was surprised. He watched it carefully after that – and soon he saw that something else was growing from the acorn, too. It was a green shoot that grew upwards, not downwards like the root.

"Well! Fancy a shoot being packed inside that tiny acorn too!" said Sammy.

The acorn liked being in the acorn-glass. It grew such a long root that it touched the bottom of the vase. The shoot grew high. It opened into leaves!

Time went on, and Sammy had to take the acorn out of the vase. The root and stalk were too big for the little vase!

The shell of the acorn still stuck to the plant. Sammy couldn't imagine how such a big root and shoot could have come from the tiny acorn.

"Well, there must be very powerful magic inside acorns," he said. "Mummy, can I plant it in the garden?"

"Yes, do," said Mummy. So Sammy took it out and planted the acorn tree at the side of the lawn. It liked being there. The rain came to it and the sun shone down on it and the wind blew the little tuft of leaves about. It grew and grew and grew.

In three years' time it was as tall as Sammy! Still the magic in it went on and on, and the little tree grew higher and thicker. When winter came, the tree dropped its leaves one by one – but in May new buds put out new leaves and they danced in the wind.

"That's magic too," Sammy thought, as he watched the fresh green leaves press out of the tight brown buds. "Who puts the leaves there and tells them to grow in the springtime – and to fall off in the autumn? Good gracious – the tree is taller than Mummy now!"

So it was – a beautiful little tree with a thick mass of oak leaves. It grew and it grew. Sammy grew too. He became a big boy. He became a man. He left his home and went away to get married. He came back to live at his home with his wife. He had three little children of his own.

They loved the oak tree and played under it. Then they grew up too, and went away to be married – and soon *their* little children came to play in the garden where the oak tree grew!

The tree was enormous now. Its trunk was fat and brown and strong.

Its branches were wide. It was so thick with leaves that when the red squirrel hid there he could not be seen.

Sammy had grown too; he was a grandfather now – a jolly old man with red cheeks, eyes just as brown as ever, and a ready smile. He had a seat put under his oak tree, and there he told stories to his grandchildren.

And they, too, always loved to hear tales of magic, and were always looking for spells and fairies and witches, just as Sammy used to, years and years ago.

And do you know what Sammy says to them? He says, "My dears, once I had a magic acorn – and in it was this very oak tree we are sitting underneath! There's magic for you! And what's more, I can show you the very acorn-shell that this tree was in."

And then Sammy brings out a little black box, and inside are pieces of acorn-shell – the acorn-shell belonging to the very same acorn that the old lady had given him so many, many years ago. The children all stare at it in wonder.

"But I don't believe it!" says one. "No oak tree could be in that tiny acorn-shell!"

"Ah – *I* said I didn't believe it once," says Sammy. "I was wrong – for here's the tree that was in it. And if you want to see the magic working, well, just plant an acorn yourselves, and see the tree come out of it! The best kind of magic works slowly and secretly – and you can watch it working. You take one of my tree's acorns and watch the magic in it!"

Can *you* find an acorn? Bring one home and put it into an acorn-glass or in an ordinary plant-pot. Then you, too, will see the magic working, and will get an oak-tree out of an acorn for yourself. But do keep the old acorn-shell to show your grandchildren, won't you!

The talking shoes

Once there was a little girl called Jennifer. She walked a mile to school each day and back, and that was quite a long way. Sometimes it rained and then she took her mac. Sometimes it was cold and she took her coat – and sometimes it was very hot and she wore no coat at all, but a shady hat in case she got sunstroke.

One day she set out in the sunshine. It was a nice, sunny, autumn day. Jennifer had a short coat on, and her lace-up shoes, and her school hat. She ran along, singing a song she was learning at school.

Half-way to school a great black cloud came up and it began to pour with rain. How it poured! You should have seen it. The rain came down like slanting lines of silver, and big puddles came all along the road.

Jennifer stood under a tree to shelter herself. When the rain stopped she ran out into the road again – and stepped right into a most enormous puddle! It was deeper than her ankles – so she wetted her shoes and socks dreadfully.

"Good gracious!" said Jennifer, in

dismay. "Now look what I've done! I shall have to sit in school with wet shoes and socks all morning, and I shall get an awful cold."

She walked along very sadly, thinking of how she would sneeze and cough the next day – and then she passed by a little yellow cottage where a dear old lady lived all alone. The old lady was shaking the crumbs off her tablecloth for the birds in the garden, and she called to Jennifer, who knew her well.

"Did you get caught in that rainstorm, my dear?"

"Yes, I did," said Jennifer sadly. "And just look at my shoes and socks! I stepped into a puddle, and they are wet through!"

"Dear me, that's very dangerous," said the old woman at once. "Come along in and I'll see if I can lend you a pair of my stockings, and a dry pair of shoes. I have a very small foot, so maybe I can manage something for you."

So Jennifer went into the tidy little cottage, and the old lady found a pair of lace-up shoes for Jennifer, and a pair of stockings.

"There!" she said. "These will do nicely. I can lend you a pair of garters, too, to keep up the stockings. Put them on, my dear, and I will dry your wet things and have them ready for you by the time you pass by at dinner-time."

Jennifer put on the stockings. Then she put on the shoes. They had big tongues to them, and long laces, but they were most comfortable. They felt nice and dry too.

"Thank you," said Jennifer gratefully. "I'll try not to tread in any more puddles with these on."

She skipped off to school. The old lady stood at the gate and called after her. "Oh – Jennifer dear – just a minute. Don't be naughty at school today, will you? You may be sorry if you are!"

"How funny!" thought Jennifer. "Why should I have to be specially good today? *I* don't know."

Jennifer was not very good at school. She whispered and talked when she shouldn't. She made a mess in her writing book instead of keeping it nice and tidy. She pulled the plaits of the little girl in front, and she pinched the boy next to her because she didn't like him. So you see she really wasn't a very good child at school.

She didn't see any real reason why she should be good that day. So she didn't try. She picked up her number book so roughly that a page tore in half.

Then a funny thing happened. A voice spoke in the silence of the classroom — a rather deepdown, husky voice that no one had ever heard before.

"Careless girl, isn't she?" said the voice. "Did you see how she tore her number book?"

"Yes, I did," said another voice, just as deepdown and husky. "She ought to lose a mark for that."

"Who is talking?" asked Miss Brown in astonishment, looking round the class. The voices didn't sound a bit like any of the girls' voices. The children stared round in amazement. Jennifer went red. How dare somebody talk about her like that?

She wondered if it was the little boy next to her. She pinched him slyly. A voice spoke loudly again.

"Did you see Jennifer pinch the little boy next to her? Isn't she cruel?"

"A most unkind child," said the second voice. "I don't think I like her."

"Oh! Who's talking like that about me!" cried Jennifer in a rage.

"It sounds like somebody on the ground," said Miss Brown, puzzled and alarmed. Everyone looked on the floor. Nobody was hiding beneath the tables or desks.

Have you guessed what it was that was talking? Perhaps you have! It was the tongues in the two borrowed shoes! They chattered away to one another, and were most surprising to hear.

"I think she has a very cross face, don't you?" said one tongue. "It's a pity she doesn't look in the mirror. Then she would see how horrid she looks when she keeps frowning."

"Will you stop talking, whoever it is?" cried Miss Brown, and she rapped on her desk.

The shoes held their tongues and stopped talking for a while. They were frightened of Miss Brown. The class settled down to write. They were copying from the blackboard. Jennifer did not try very hard. When she opened her desk to get out her pen her book slid to the floor.

"Good gracious!" said one tongue to the other. "Just look at Jennifer's dreadful writing! Did you ever see anything so awful for a child of ten?

Really, she ought to be ashamed of herself."

"Poor thing! Perhaps she can't write any better," said the other tongue, flapping itself a little. "Look at that mistake! If I were the teacher, I would put Jennifer into the corner."

"Oh! Oh!" cried Jennifer, stamping her foot and bursting into tears. "I won't stand it! Who is saying these horrid things about me?"

"I can't imagine, Jenny," said Miss Brown. "All I can say is that the things are perfectly true! It is a shocking thing that a girl of ten should write so badly and be so untidy."

Jennifer picked up her book sulkily and put it on her desk. The shoes chatted together again.

"She's got her horrid, sulky face on now. Isn't she a most unpleasant child? I wonder how many mistakes she will make on her next page!"

Jennifer set her teeth and made up her mind to make no mistakes at all. She wrote a really beautiful page and showed it to Miss Brown.

"Good gracious, Jennifer! I've never seen such nice writing from you before!" cried Miss Brown.

"You see, she *can* do it if she tries," said one shoe. "She's just too lazy to do it always."

"I'm not lazy, I'm not lazy!" cried Jennifer, and she stamped her foot. That gave the shoes such a shock that they said nothing at all for a whole hour. Then it was geography, a lesson that Jennifer didn't like. She leaned over and pulled the plaits of the little girl in front of her. The little girl squealed.

"Somebody pulled my hair!" she cried.

Miss Brown looked up crossly.

"Was it you, Jenny?" she asked.

"No, Miss Brown," said Jennifer untruthfully.

"OooooooooooOOOOOH!" said one shoe to the other. "Isn't she untruthful? Really! Ooooooooh!"

"Untruthful, cowardly and unkind," said the other shoe. "Why doesn't somebody send her to bed?"

Jennifer glared round at everyone, thinking that *somebody* must be playing a trick on her, talking like this. But everyone was as astonished as she was.

"Who *is* talking?" cried Miss Brown, quite alarmed again. "I don't like this. I shall put the talkers into the corner if I hear any more."

"Fancy! She'd put us in the corner!" giggled a shoe. "Well, she'd have to put Jenny there, too, if she put us."

"Perhaps we'd better not talk," said the other shoe. "I believe we are disturbing the class a little. Sh!"

So they said no more until it was time to go home. Then Jennifer went sulkily to the cloakroom and took down her hat and coat. Another child got in her way, and she gave him a push that knocked him right over.

"Isn't she rough?" said the shoe,

shocked. "Did you see her push that nice little boy right over? If she did that to me, I'd kick her!"

"And I'd trip her up!" said the other shoe fiercely. "Horrid girl! Do you suppose anyone in the world likes her at all?"

"I expect her mother does," said the first shoe. "Mothers are funny – they always love their children even when the children are horrid and rude to them. I should think Jennifer is rude to her mother, wouldn't you?"

Jenny sat down on a bench and began to cry. "I'm *not* rude to my mother, I'm not, I'm not," she wept. "I love her. I'm kind to her. Oh, who is it saying these unkind things about me? I may behave horribly sometimes, but I *can* be good when I try!"

"I don't believe that, do you?" said one shoe.

"No," said the other. "She couldn't be good! She's one of these spoilt children we've heard about."

The other children laughed. They were sorry for Jennifer, but they couldn't help thinking that it would do her good to hear these things. She went off crying bitterly, puzzled and unhappy.

The shoes talked on and on. They chatted about Jenny's bad writing and her wrong sums and her pinching and pushing. Jenny sobbed and cried all the way to the little yellow cottage. The old lady was waiting for her at the gate.

"Dear, dear!" she said, when she saw Jenny coming along with red eyes and tear-stained cheeks. "What's the matter? Have those shoes been wagging their tongues too much?"

"Shoes? Wagging their tongues?" said Jenny in amazement. "What do you mean?"

"Well, those shoes I lent you this morning can be most tiresome," said the old lady. "They belonged to my great-grandmother, you know, and were made by a brownie, so it is said. They have tongues, of course, just as your own lace-up shoes have – but these shoe tongues can talk – and talk they do! They are real chatterboxes. I hope they didn't say anything unkind!"

"Oh, no, we only spoke the truth!" cried the two shoe tongues together, and they flapped themselves about in the shoes. Jenny looked down in amazement. She took off the shoes very quickly indeed.

"So they were the talkers!" she said. "The tongues of my shoes! Well – I never knew shoe tongues could talk!"

"Oh, my dear, they all could at one time," said the old lady. "That is why they were called tongues, you know, because they spoke. But they did say the silliest, most tiresome things, so now very few of them are allowed to talk. I can't stop the tongues in this pair of shoes, though.

That's why I called to you to be good this morning – because I knew the shoe tongues would talk about it if you were naughty."

"I shan't be *quite* so naughty in future," said Jenny, beginning to smile. "I don't like to be thought lazy and stupid and horrid. Lend me your shoes in a month's time, and see if they can say heaps of *nice* things about me for a change, will you?"

"Certainly," said the old lady, slipping Jenny's own shoes on her feet. "How cross they will be if there is nothing naughty they can chat about!"

I'd like to hear what they say in a month's time, wouldn't you? What would *your* shoe tongues say if they could speak, I wonder? Do tell me!

The Gossamer Elf

Everybody knew the Gossamer Elf. She was the cleverest dressmaker in the whole of Fairyland. You should have seen the dresses and cloaks she made!

"I think her autumn clothes are the best," said Winks. "She made me a lovely dress last October of a red creeper leaf. I went to lots of parties in it."

"She made me a cloak out of a pair of beech leaves," said Feefo. "It was a golden cloak, the prettiest I ever had."

"Her stitches are the finest I ever saw," said Tiptoe. "Well – they're so fine I can't see them! Once I thought

149

that the Gossamer Elf didn't sew our frocks at all, but just made them by magic. She doesn't though; I've seen her sewing away with a tiny, tiny needle."

"Ah, but have you seen her thread?" said Winks. "It's so fine and so strong that once she's put a stitch into a dress it never comes undone."

"What does she use for thread?" said Feefo. "I'd like to get some. I'll go and ask her."

So she went to call on the Gossamer Elf. But the Elf was out. She had left her door open and Feefo went inside. On a shelf she saw reels upon reels – but they were all empty. Not one reel had any thread on it. How strange!

Soon the Gossamer Elf came in. Feefo ran to her. "I've come to ask you something. Where do you get your fine thread? I can't see any on your reels."

The Gossamer Elf smiled. "No – my reels are all empty now," she said. "But soon they will be filled again with the finest, silkiest thread. I always get my thread at this time of year, you know."

"Where from?" asked Feefo. "Can I get some too? Do let me. Take me with you and I'll buy some."

"I don't buy it," said the Elf. "Yes, you can come with me if you like. I'm starting out tomorrow morning at dawn. You can carry some of my empty reels with you. That will be a help."

So Feefo and the Gossamer Elf set out at dawn. They went to the fields. It was a lovely morning, and the sun shone softly from a blue sky.

"It's gossamer time now," said the Elf. "Did you know that? Soon the air will be full of fine silken threads that will stretch across the fields everywhere. See – you can spy some already, gleaming in the sun."

Feefo looked. Yes – she could see some fine, long threads stretching from

the hedge above high up into the air.
Soon there would be plenty of them.

"But what are those silky threads?"
said Feefo in wonder. "Where do they
come from? Who makes them?"

"Climb up the hedge with me and
I'll show you," said the Elf. "Some
very small friends of mine make them.
We'll watch them."

They climbed up the hedge together,
using the prickles on the wild rose
stems as steps. They soon got high up
in the hedge. Then Feefo saw around
her many tiny spiders – young ones,
not much more than babies.

Some stood on leaves, some clung
to stems, and all of them were doing
the same thing. They were sending out
long silken threads from underneath
their bodies.

"They have their silk spinnerets
there," said the Elf. "Big spiders have
too. They take the thread from their
spinnerets. Watch that tiny spider.
See the long thread coming out, and

waving in the air?"

"Oh, yes," said Feefo, in surprise. She saw dozens of tiny spiders all doing the same thing. "But why are they all doing this, Elf? It seems very strange to me. They are not spinning webs."

"No, they are going out into the world to seek their fortunes," said the Elf. "Each baby spider wants to leave the place where he was born. He wants to journey far away and find his own place to live. So he is sending out a long, long thread into the air – and then, when he has a long enough line, he will let the wind take him off into the air with his gossamer thread – and, like a tiny parachutist, he will soar over the world, and then drop gently to ground."

"Goodness me!" said Feefo, astonished. "Look, there goes one, Elf! Away he goes on the wind."

The tiny spider had let go his hold of the leaf, and now, swinging gently on the end of his gossamer thread, he let himself be carried away on the breeze, exactly like a tiny parachutist. Feefo and the Elf watched him soaring away, until he could no longer be seen.

"They're all doing it, all the baby spiders!" cried Feefo in delight. "Oh, look at them swinging away on their threads. The wind blows the threads away and the spiders go with them!"

They watched the curious sight for a little while. Then Feefo turned to the Elf. "But, Elf," she said, "surely you don't take their threads away from the tiny spiders? That would be a most unkind thing to do."

"Of course I don't," said the Elf. "How could you think I'd do that? No – once the spiders have made their journey and landed safely somewhere, they don't want their threads any more. So I collect them on my reels, you see. I wind them up carefully, and soon have all my reels full for my year's work."

"Well, what a good idea," cried Feefo. "Look – here comes a spider from far away; see him swinging down on the end of his line? Here he is, just beside us. Little spider, what an adventure you've had!"

"May I take your thread please, if you don't want it any more?" asked the Gossamer Elf politely. "Oh, thank you. What a nice long one!"

She began to wind the gossamer round and round her reel. Soon the reel was full. The spider ran off to find himself a nice new home under a leaf. Maybe he would catch plenty of flies there, he thought. Soon he would spin a fine web, and wait for his dinner to come along and fly into it.

Another spider landed a little farther down. Feefo ran to him. As soon as he had cast off his gossamer she began to wind it round and round the reel she carried. "What fun this is!" she thought. "Now I know why the Gossamer Elf has her name. How clever she is to think of this idea!"

Day after day, early in the morning, Feefo and the Gossamer Elf came out together and waited for the adventuring spiders to land near them on their gossamer lines. Soon they had dozens and dozens of reels full of the fine silken thread.

"There. We've got enough!" said the Elf at last. "Now I shall wait for the leaves to change colour, and soon I shall be hard at work again making winter dresses and cloaks and sewing them with the gossamer thread given me by the tiny spiders. I shall be very busy indeed this winter!"

So she is. She is making coats of blackberry leaves, crimson, yellow and pink; frocks of golden hazel leaves, trimmed with berries, and cloaks of brilliant cherry leaves. You should see them! But you can't see her stitches – they are made of the gossamer from the spiders.

Have you ever seen it? You really must. You can take some too, if you want, for the spiders won't need it again.

The magic bubble pipes

M erry and Bright were hard at work making their famous bubble pipes. They were pretty little pipes, carved neatly round the bowl, and the brownies sold them for a penny each. Merry and Bright sold hundreds of them, for the fairies loved to blow bubbles. Sometimes the little people sailed off on a big one, and sometimes they took their little scissors and snipped pieces off the brightest coloured bubbles to make into dresses and coats.

Now one day Dame Tiptap came along and looked at the little pipes. She didn't want to buy one, but she liked to stand and watch the two little

brownies making them.

Merry and Bright thought she was a funny old dame.

"Do you want a pipe to smoke, Dame Tiptap?" asked Merry.

"Of course not," said the old lady angrily. "You know I would never dream of smoking a pipe. Don't be rude!"

"Have a look at this one, Dame Tiptap," said Bright, and he held up a long-stemmed pipe to the old lady. It was filled with soapy water, but Dame Tiptap didn't know that. She put on her glasses to have a look, for she thought the pipe must be a special one.

"Smell it," said Bright, with a giggle. Dame Tiptap bent closer and smelled it, and at that very moment Bright blew hard down the stem of the pipe, and some soapy bubbles rose out of the bowl and burst in the old lady's face. What a fright she got! She nearly fell over, and how those two rascally brownies roared to see her face covered all over with bubbles.

"That is very rude and unkind of you," said Dame Tiptap angrily. "You deserve to be punished for that." She took out a yellow box, and from it scattered a misty powder over the brownies' hands.

"There's a spell in that," she said, "and it's gone into your fingers now. Whatever you make will get a bit of the spell too, when the powder works. Ha, ha, Merry and Bright, you'll soon wish you hadn't played a trick on old Tiptap!"

Off she went, wiping her soapy face. The brownies looked at one another in dismay, and then looked at their hands. They seemed all right. Whatever could the spell be?

"Oh, it's just nothing," said Merry at last. "She was trying to frighten us, that's all."

They went on with their work and made dozens of bubble pipes that day, but the spell went into many of the pipes as they worked, and lay there until the right time came.

Twelve of the pipes had the spell. The rest were all right. The little people came to buy the pipes and took them home. They made soapy water and put the pipes to their mouths, and blew bubbles.

And then those pipes that had the spell in them began to act very strangely indeed! Even when the fairy stopped blowing, the soapy bubbles went on coming out of the pipe! Soon the room was full of bubbles, but still the pipe went on blowing them out. They floated out of the window. They floated through the wood, and then, one by one, they burst.

And, dear me, each bubble burst with a bang as loud as a gun going off. It made everyone jump nearly out of their skins, and the King cried, "Guns! Is that an enemy coming?"

Bang! Bang! Bang! The bubbles went

on bursting as they flew out of the pipes. The King and his courtiers sent orders to the army to turn out. It must be an enemy coming! Bang! BANG!

The army turned out, and aeroplanes buzzed overhead to see if they could find the enemy with so many guns. But not a sign of anyone could they see. Just then some of the bubbles, which had floated high in the air, burst near the aeroplanes. Bang! Bang! Pop! Bang!

"We are being shot at!" cried the pilots, and they raced downwards to tell the King. What a to-do there was! All that day, as the bubbles popped and banged, messengers rushed here and there trying to find out what was the matter, and the army marched north, south, east and west to stop the enemy that nobody could see.

And then, at last, bubbles floated into the palace garden, and the King saw that what he had thought was the banging of guns was really the popping of magic bubbles. How annoyed he was.

To think he had called out his army and his air force to fight a lot of bubbles!

It wasn't long before he had Merry and Bright before him and was asking them the meaning of such a thing. They were trembling, because they had not known that the spell would cause the pipes to go on pouring out bubbles, bubbles that banged like guns when they burst.

They told the King everything, and he sent for Dame Tiptap too. Merry and Bright felt ashamed of themselves when the old lady told of the trick they had played on her.

"You should not have blown such a powerful spell over their hands," said the King. "It has caused a great deal of trouble. Take the spell off their hands, Dame Tiptap."

"I can't, Your Majesty," said the old lady. "It is there for good."

"Well, they will have to put up with it, then," said the King. "But I doubt if anyone will buy their pipes now that they know what dreadful bubbles they blow. Take the magic pipes, Dame Tiptap, and destroy them. We cannot have them pouring out bubbles like this."

So the pipes were burnt, and the bang-bang-bang of bursting bubbles stopped. There was peace once more.

But Merry and Bright found that the King was right when he said that no one would want to buy their pipes any more. Everyone was too much afraid of getting an enchanted pipe. They didn't want that! So they went to the yellow goblin, who also sold pipes, and bought them from him, and Merry and Bright found that they were getting very poor indeed.

"What shall we do?" said Merry. But Bright didn't know. The two brownies could not do anything else but make pipes. They sat and looked as miserable as could be.

And then an old oak tree near by spoke to them.

"I will buy your pipes to put my acorns in," said the tree. "But as I have about a thousand acorns this year, I cannot pay you a penny for each of your pipes. I shall give you one penny for a hundred pipes. That's all."

"But we should have to work dreadfully, dreadfully hard then!" cried Merry.

"Hard work never hurt anyone," said the oak tree. "Well, take it or leave it. You'll find no one else buys your pipes now, and it surely is better to sell them at a penny a hundred than to have them falling to bits in your cupboard!"

Well, there was some sense in what the tree said, and the two brownies had to agree. But how hard they had to work now – and for such a little money too! They made the little pipes all day long, and at night they set the acorns neatly into them, so that each acorn had a little resting-place and did not easily fall off the tree when the wind blew. The oak tree made them carve the pipes neatly, just as before.

Merry and Bright are not quite so merry and bright now! But still, as the oak tree said, hard work never hurt anyone; and although the two brownies haven't nearly so much money as they used to have, they still have time to play now and again. You will usually see them in an oak wood, hard at work on their tiny pipes; and it is said that some of the pipes have that magic spell in them still, so if you want a bit of excitement, try blowing bubbles through a few of the acorn pipes and see if anything happens. You never know!

And don't forget to see how neatly Merry and Bright carve the bowls of their pipes, and how beautifully they make them to fit each acorn.

The Christmas pudding wish

"**C**hildren! I'm making your Christmas pudding!" called Mummy. "It's all mixed. Do you want to come and stir it round, and wish your Christmas wish?"

"Oh *yes!*" shouted the three children and they came rushing into the kitchen. Mummy had a big bowl and in it was a glorious mixture. Big Peter took the spoon first and stirred hard. He wished hard too.

Then Alice stirred and wished. "And now it's your turn, Little Ben," said Mummy. Ben really was very small indeed. He had been ill a great many times and he just hadn't grown.

"Will my wish really come true?" he said.

"You never know!" said his mother. "Wish your very hardest!"

So Ben stirred the stiff mixture and he wished a wish to himself. "I wish I could see Father Christmas and help him!" He wished it three times for luck.

Now, on Christmas Eve the three children hung up their stockings, of course. Ben's was smaller than anyone's because his feet were tiny. He didn't think Father Christmas would be able to put much into it!

He went to bed – but he kept thinking of his Christmas pudding wish. *Would* it come true? Did pudding wishes ever come true?

"I must keep awake," thought Ben. "I can't expect my wish to come true if I'm asleep when Father Christmas comes!"

About twelve o'clock, when the house was dark and still, Ben went to the window. He thought he had heard a faraway jingling of bells. Yes – he had. And will you believe it, four reindeer came galloping through the sky, their bells jingling merrily. Ben watched in excitement.

And then, just as the sleigh was over Ben's garden, something fell out – something small that went tumbling down into the thick snow just outside Ben's window! Whatever could it be?

Then the reindeer stopped with a jerk, and to Ben's enormous delight the sleigh came down to earth in his garden – and in the moonlight he saw the big, burly figure of Father Christmas!

Father Christmas got out and went over to the little thing in the snow. "Are you hurt?" Ben heard him say. "Dear, dear – how silly of you to fall out like that!"

Ben was so excited that he began to shake. He must go and speak to Father Christmas, he must, he must! He pulled on his dressing-gown, tied a scarf round

his neck, and slipped down the stairs and out of the garden door. Soon he stood beside Father Christmas.

"Hallo there!" said Father Christmas, surprised. "What a tiny thing you are! Are you a pixie or something?"

"No. I'm a boy," said Ben. "What's happened?"

"A most annoying thing," said Father Christmas. "I brought this little imp with me to go down the chimneys instead of me this year. Somehow or other I've got a bit plump, and I'm afraid of getting stuck. And now the silly little creature has fallen out and hurt himself – he says he can't go climbing up and down chimneys tonight. And I'd like to know where I can get anyone small enough at a moment's notice!"

Well! *Ben* knew where he could get someone! He pulled at Father Christmas's sleeve. "Won't *I* do?" he said anxiously. "See how small I am! I could go down chimneys easily. Let me help you, do, do let me help you!"

"Right," said Father Christmas. "It's very good of you. Change clothes with the imp. He's got a black suit on, so that the soot won't show."

In two minutes Ben had the black suit on, and was sitting beside Father Christmas in the sleigh. What a treat! What a surprise! His Christmas pudding wish had come true!

Well, Ben found it easy to slip down chimneys and climb up again. He was very good and quick at stuffing stockings full of toys. He chuckled when he saw the sleeping children. What would they say if they woke up and saw who was filling their stockings *that* night?

He even filled Big Peter's stocking, and Alice's. But he didn't fill his own. He didn't quite like to do that. Anyway, what did it matter if his was empty in the morning? He would have had the most wonderful treat in the world!

Ben was very busy that night. The roofs they landed on! The chimneys he went down! The big and little stockings he filled! Father Christmas was delighted with him.

"Don't grow too big next year," he said. "I might want you again! Now – we've finished. Here we are back in your garden again. Change clothes with the imp."

They changed clothes. Ben rubbed the soft nose of each reindeer, gave Father Christmas a sudden hug and ran in through the garden door and up the stairs. He was very tired.

"I'm happy, I'm happy!" he said to himself as he got into bed. "Nobody will believe me tomorrow – but it's quite, quite true!"

In the morning what a surprise! Ben sat up in bed and the first thing he saw was his stocking full with toys from top to toe. They overflowed on to the bed and even on to the floor! He sat and stared at them.

Had he dreamt it all then? His stocking had been empty when he climbed into bed. Surely the imp hadn't been able to get down the chimney after all?

"I don't believe my wish *did* come true," thought Ben, sadly. "I've just had a lovely dream. Oh, I *do* feel so disappointed!"

But wait – what was this? Ben, Ben, look at your hands! Black with soot! Where did *that* come from? Ben gave a squeal of joy.

"It *was* true! I've helped Father Christmas – and somehow my stocking has been filled too! It's ALL true!"

Wasn't it strange the way his Christmas pudding wish came true? Do you ever wish when you stir the Christmas pudding? You do? Well, let me know if your wish comes true, like Ben's, won't you?

I do hope it does.

Go and dig potatoes!

Once, when little Dame Hurry was walking over the common with her shopping in a basket, she heard a lark singing. It was singing so beautifully that she looked up to see where it was.

"Your music pours down like rain!" she called to the lark. She hurried on her way, still looking up at the singing lark, high in the blue sky. She didn't see a rabbit-hole. She put her little foot right into it and fell over.

She gave a scream. "Oh, my ankle, my ankle! I've sprained it. Oh, the pain! Help, help!"

Poor little Dame Hurry sat on the grass and nursed her foot. She couldn't stand on it because it hurt her so. All her shopping was spilt from her basket. Dear, dear, and her Aunt Lollipop was coming to dinner.

"Help!" called Dame Hurry, hoping that someone would hear her. "Help!"

Somebody did hear her. It was Grabbit the Goblin. He came over to Dame Hurry, and she told him what she had done. "Could you help me home, please?" she asked. "And pick up my shopping for me?"

"I shall want something in return for my trouble," said Grabbit, who was mean and unkind.

"Oh, can't you help me just out of kindness?" said Dame Hurry. "It's so much nicer to do things for that reason, if you can."

"Pooh! Kindness! Not me," said Grabbit rudely. "Well, if you can't give me a reward for helping you, I'm off. No one else is likely to come by today, so you'll be here all day – and all night, too, I shouldn't wonder!"

"How mean you are," said Dame Hurry. "But don't go, please don't go. I really must get home before my Aunt Lollipop comes. I'll give you ten pence for your trouble."

"No, I don't want that," said Grabbit, looking suddenly very sly. "I want something else. Lend me your magic spade for a week."

"Certainly not!" said Dame Hurry. "What, lend my precious magic to *you*? I wouldn't dream of it."

"Right, then! I'm going," said Grabbit, and took a step away. Dame Hurry began to cry. "All right, all right, you mean creature. I'll lend you my spade for a week, and much good may it do you!"

"It will!" said Grabbit. "It can dig up all my potatoes for me! Ho, ho! It will save me a lot of work, I can tell you."

He helped Dame Hurry to her feet, after he had picked up her shopping. Then he helped her home. Her Aunt Lollipop had already arrived, and ran to bathe Dame Hurry's poor swollen foot.

"What about that spade?" said Grabbit. "I want it now."

"Oh dear, oh dear, can't you even wait till my foot is bathed?" said Dame Hurry. "Well, you will find it in the garden shed. But, listen, Grabbit, you will have to speak to the spade politely and kindly, and you must always clean it when it has been working for you."

"Pooh!" said Grabbit, rudely, and went off to get the spade. It was rather a peculiar one, for it had no proper handle, but a very big steel piece for digging. Grabbit picked it up, put it over his shoulder, and went home.

He stuck the spade into the ground. "Go and dig potatoes," he commanded. The spade hopped over to a potato patch and set to work. It was marvellous to see it digging away by itself.

"Hey! Sort the potatoes out nicely," said Grabbit to the spade. "Don't fling them here, there and everywhere. Big ones together, and middle-sized ones, and small ones, do you hear?"

The spade dug so violently that one of the potatoes shot up in the air and hit Grabbit on the head. He growled and went indoors.

The spade finished digging up that patch of potatoes. It hopped into the kitchen to be cleaned. But Grabbit wasn't going to bother to do that!

"Go and stand in the shed," he ordered the spade. "*I'm* not going to bother to clean you."

The spade hopped out, making a tremendous noise as if it was cross. Grabbit went to sleep.

Next day he ordered the spade to dig up a weedy patch of garden for him. "And do it properly!" he said. "Get the weeds up by the roots. Go on, dig!"

The spade dug. It flung up the weeds so high that bits of earth flew all over Grabbit. He went indoors, frowning. As soon as he had gone into the house the spade went over to the fence and leaned itself there. It didn't do any more digging at all.

When Grabbit came out and found that the spade had done hardly any digging, he lost his temper. "I'll put you on the rubbish heap! You'll do what I say or you'll be sorry!"

He didn't clean the spade that day, either. It went to its place in the shed so dirty that there wasn't one single shiny bit to be seen. It scraped itself angrily along the floor.

The next day, Grabbit wanted to go and do some shopping. He called to the spade first. "Go and dig potatoes! Dig and dig and dig! Don't you dare to stop digging once you begin. Go and dig potatoes!"

The spade hopped out to a very big potato patch and began to dig. It was afraid of Grabbit. Suppose he really did put it on the rubbish heap?

Grabbit went out shopping. He met some friends and was a very long time gone. The spade dug up all the potatoes and sorted them out carefully.

Then it wondered where Grabbit was and went to look for him in the kitchen. No Grabbit. Well, well, Grabbit had told the spade to dig and dig and dig, and not stop, so the spade thought it had better obey.

It went out into the garden and dug up all the rose-trees. Then it dug up the onions. Then it went to the lawn and dug up all the grass.

Well, there was no garden to dig after that. What could the spade do next? It had to dig and dig and dig!

It dug up the fence. That was a hard job, and the spade enjoyed it. Then it dug up the garden shed. My, that was a fine job for a magic spade! It dug so hard that it almost panted.

Still Grabbit wasn't back. So the spade began to dig up Grabbit's cottage. It dug and it dug, heaving itself

underneath it, and soon the cottage began to topple over on one side. The spade was pleased.

Then Grabbit came back. He was shocked to see his cottage toppling over. He was horrified to see his garden shed lying on its side. He couldn't believe his eyes when he saw his fence dug up – and his lawn – and his roses. He must be in a dream!

But he wasn't. It was quite, quite true. He rushed at the hard-working spade with a shout – but it hopped away at once, and went back to Dame Hurry.

Grabbit went crying round to Dame Hurry, too. "Come and see the damage your horrid magic spade has done. It has dug up my fence and shed and my house, too! You'll have to pay me for all that!"

"Indeed I shan't," said Dame Hurry. "You can put everything right yourself. It's all your own fault. And if you say another word, I'll *give* you the spade, Grabbit – and maybe it will start digging you up, too!"

"I wish I'd helped you out of kindness now," wept Grabbit. "I wish I had. I wouldn't have brought all this trouble on myself then."

"Ah, no luck comes to those who have to be paid for doing a bit of kindness," said Dame Hurry. "No luck at all. Just you remember that, Grabbit."

183

The Ho-Ho goblins

O nce upon a time the Ho-Ho goblins laid a plan. They wanted to catch the Skippetty pixies, but for a long time they hadn't been able even to get near them. Now they had thought of a marvellous idea!

"Listen!" said Snicky, the head goblin. "You know when the pixies sit down to feast, in the middle of their dancing, don't you? Well, they sit on toadstools! And if *we* grow those toadstools we can put a spell in them so that as soon as the pixies sit down on them, they shoot through the earth into our caves below – and we shall have captured them."

"A splendid idea!" said the other

goblins in delight. "We'll do it!"

"Leave it all to me," said Snicky. "I will go to them and offer to grow them toadstools for their dance much more cheaply than anyone else."

He went knocking at the door of Pinky, one of the chief pixies.

"Dear Madam Pinky," said Snicky, bowing low, "I come to ask you if you will kindly allow me to grow the toadstools for you for your dance."

"How much do you charge?" asked Pinky.

"One gold piece for one hundred toadstools," said Snicky.

"That is very cheap," said Pinky. "Very well. You shall make them."

Snicky ran off full of glee. He had got what he wanted! He called a meeting of the others, and told them.

"Now," he said, "not one of you must tell a word of this to anyone, for we must keep it a secret. We must get a runaway spell from Witch Grumple, and each toadstool must be rubbed with the spell. Then, at a magic word, all the toadstools, with the pixies on them, will rush away through the ground straight to our caves below."

"Hurrah!" cried the Ho-Ho goblins. "They will be our servants at last."

Snicky went to ask Witch Grumple for the spell.

"Good evening, Witch Grumple," said Snicky. "May I speak secretly with you for a moment?"

"Certainly," said the witch. She looked all around to see that no one was about. "Come into the corn," she said. "No one will hear us then. What is it you want?"

"I want a runaway spell," said Snicky.

"What will you give me for it?" asked the witch.

"I'll give you two Skippetty pixies for servants," said Snicky.

"Don't be silly," said Grumple. "You haven't any pixies to give away!"

"I soon shall have if you let me have the runaway spell," said Snicky.

"Tell me what you are going to do with it," said Grumple.

"No," said Snicky, "someone might hear me."

"There is no one to hear you," said Grumple. "Tell me, or I will not let you have the spell."

So Snicky told Grumple exactly what he was going to do to capture the pixies, and she shook with laughter.

"Splendid!" she said. "I shall be glad to see those stuck-up little pixies punished. Come back with me and I'll give you the spell."

Now all would have gone well with the Ho-Ho goblin's plan – if someone hadn't overheard the secret that Snicky told Grumple. Who heard it? You will never guess.

The corn heard it with their many, many ears! They listened to all that Snicky said, and, because they liked the Skippetty pixies, they wanted to warn them. So the next time the wind blew the corn, it whispered its secret to the breeze.

"Shish-a-shish-a-shish-a-shish!" went the corn as the wind blew over it. The wind understood its language and listened in astonishment to the tale the corn told of Snicky's plan. Off it went to the pixies at once.

When Pinky heard of Snicky's plan, she went pale with rage and fear. To think how that horrid, horrid goblin had nearly tricked her! Off she sped to the Fairy King and told him everything. He laughed and said, "Aha! Now we shall be able to play a nice little trick on Snicky himself!"

So, on the night of the dance, all the pixies laughed and talked as if they had no idea of the toadstool trick. The goblins crept around, watching and waiting for the moment when they could send the toadstools rushing down below to their caves.

Suddenly Pinky stopped the dance and said, "Let's play musical chairs for a change! Goblins, come and play with us!"

Pinky pointed to the toadstools that Snicky had grown for them.

"Those shall be the chairs," she said. "When the music stops, everyone must sit down if he can!"

The band began again. Pixies and goblins ran merrily round the toadstools – but every pixie had been warned not to sit down, but to let the goblins take the toadstools. So, when the music stopped, the goblins made a rush for the toadstools and sat down on them.

As soon as Pinky saw the goblins sitting on the toadstools, she called out a magic word at the top of her voice. Those toadstools sank down through the ground at top speed!

To the goblins' great fright, the toadstools rushed down to their cave – and there, calmly waiting for them, were the soldiers of the Fairy King. As the toadstools came to rest in the caves, each goblin was surrounded by three soldiers. They were prisoners!

"That was a fine trick you planned,

wasn't it?" grinned a soldier. "But not so fine when it's played on yourselves! Come along now, quick march!"

Off the goblins went – and for a whole year they had to work hard for the pixies, to punish them for trying to play such a horrid trick.

And to this day they don't know who gave their secret away – although people say that if you listen to the corn as it whispers in the wind, you can, if you have sharp ears, hear it telling the wind all about Witch Grumple and Snicky the goblin. I'd love to hear it, wouldn't you?